THE FUTURE COLLECTION

BETH REVIS

*For the giants upon whose shoulders I have stood,
particularly Philip K. Dick, Ray Bradbury,
Madeleine L'Engle & Ursula K. Le Guin*

All stories feature science fiction settings and tropes, and most involve some element of body horror or mental control and manipulation. In particular, "Lag" heavily features body horror, and "The Turing Test" heavily features mental manipulation. "The Most Precious Memory" speaks on addiction. "The Girl & the Machine" and "As They Slip Away" recount an episode of sexual assault and/or mention sexual assault and issues of consent. "Malfunction" features pregnancy loss heavily and mentions questionable consent that is not entirely explored by the character within the context of the story.

INTRODUCTION

I used to say I wasn't a short story writer. I enjoy building the world far too much, and that takes words, enough words to fill a whole novel.

But every once in awhile I'll get those flashes of ideas—the ones that are just a quick "what if *that* happened" or "what if *this* didn't happen"—and all of a sudden, a character will pop up in my mind, ready to answer that one question...but no more.

The following is a collection of short stories that did just that—they answered my "what if" questions, they explored a character or two, and then they walked off into the sunset. Some of these stories became seeds for novels—"The Turing Test" was a one-off idea that didn't let me go and became *The Body Electric.* The "girl with sunset hair" haunted me in "The Most Precious Memory" and became a feature of the main character in *Across the Universe.*

Each short story is its own tale. None of them are linked, and none of them exist outside of their few pages.

But there's something magical, I think, about a story that's limited to such a small space. I'm often reminded of Madeleine L'Engle's description of a sonnet in *A Wrinkle in Time:* Part of the beauty is in the constraints of the form, and of fitting something important within those constraints.

ONE

DOCTOR-PATIENT CONFIDENTIALITY

OPHELIA HAMILTON WOKE up all at once. There was no yawning, gentle stretching, or slow awareness of consciousness as lingering dreams faded. Her eyes opened, and she was awake.

"Ow," she said, looking down at her arm. A needle protruded from the soft skin on the inside of her elbow. Another was driven through the vein at the top of her hand. Thin, clear tape pulled at the fine hairs on her skin, keeping the needles in place.

She was in something like a capsule, with a transparent-blue rounded hood over her body. The hood slid away in two neat pieces, out of sight, and Ophelia blinked in the bright light.

"Hello," a man's voice said.

Ophelia tried to move her head but found her neck stiff and unyielding. She struggled to sit up. Her body, far too weak, failed her. Instead, the capsule she was lying in tilted up. There must be some sort of anti-grav field around the tray; she was raised to a standing position, but felt none of her own weight. She tried to take a step, but she only had the strength to do little more than float steadily within the edges of the opened capsule.

"You may be experiencing mild memory loss and disorientation," the male voice said. "Please don't be afraid."

The voice reminded her of someone, but Ophelia couldn't recall who. She strained to move her neck enough to see the speaker, but then he shifted, appearing in her line of vision.

He wore a white lab coat with a scanner sticking out of the front breast pocket and insta-gloves folded in the large pocket by his hip.

"You're a doctor," Ophelia said. Her words were slow and measured, as if she were learning how to speak with each syllable.

"I am," the doctor confirmed.

"I'm in...a hospital?"

"A cryo-med wing."

Cyro-med: Where doctors stored patients if they couldn't find a cure quick enough to save the patient's life.

"What...happened?" Ophelia's words were nearly a whisper now.

The doctor drew up a chair and sat down across from her. He slid his finger across a hard plastic shell encasing his left forearm and a screen popped up. Ophelia gaped; she'd never seen such advanced, sleek tech. She tried to read the screen but couldn't; it was dimmed on her side.

"In long-term cryo-med patients, we've learned it's

easier for the patient to adjust if she remembers her own past, rather than being told what happened. Take your time." The doctor smiled at her, the wrinkles at his eyes deepening. "Start with your name."

"Ophelia," she said instantly.

The doctor tapped on his screen. "Your whole name."

"Ophelia Lucille Hamilton."

The doctor smiled banally. He seemed kind, like her grandfather had been. His face was wrinkled, but in a sweet way that made her feel safe.

"No...no, that's not right," she said. "My name is Ophelia Yuu. I...I got married. Just...just before..." Ophelia felt dizzy, floating there before the doctor. She wished she could get up, flex her legs, move around.

"Don't rush yourself." The doctor looked a little worried, staring at the screen that showed Ophelia's stats. Her heart rate was very slow and weak; she didn't need the soft beeping near her left ear to tell her that.

"I got married just a little while ago. I was on my honeymoon."

The doctor relaxed a little and resumed recording information on the screen attached to his arm.

"Benny. His name is Benny. Does he know where I am?"

"Let's just focus on you, Ophelia."

Ophelia's head spun. Why wasn't he here with her?

Why was *she* even here? Sharp pain sliced through her head, and she winced. When she opened her eyes, the doctor was waiting for her to continue.

"Benny and I had gone to university together," Ophelia

said slowly. "First-level biology. That's where we met. I was going to be a botanist. He was hoping to be assigned to extra-solar virology."

"The study of viruses originating outside of the solar system," the doctor said. Ophelia frowned at him. She knew what Benny's area of study was. Why would he say that....

"Oh," Ophelia breathed. Because that's why she was here, in cryo-med. "Benny took me to the lab his department had worked with. That's one reason why we had our honeymoon in Greece, so he could meet the people he'd worked with in person."

"On June 17, 2132," the doctor said, consulting his notes. "Benjamin Yuu and Ophelia Hamilton Yuu visited the Athens Astrosciences Department of the UC university system."

Ophelia could see it all now, like a movie playing in her mind. Benny had been overjoyed for a chance to get his hands on the Athens materials—he wasn't supposed to go into the lab until he was officially accepted in their extra-solar virology program.

Benny had always been fascinated with that particular branch of science. While Ophelia had selected biology for her first level only because she was somewhat good at it and it was easy, Benny had been driven. His little brothers, twins, had been among the children killed in the first wave of the viral plague. When the government had originally received the probe from a planet in the Gliese system, twenty light years away, the entire world's view changed. Earth was not alone. But no one—not the Gliesians, not the humans, no one—had realized that opening the probe and discovering the first message from a species of aliens on a planet not their own would also release a rare virus onto the world.

The children died first. Then the others. Only a small percentage were susceptible to the virus, but a small percentage of 10 billion people was still several million.

The Gliese system aliens hadn't intended to start biological warfare, and for a few years, the situation was tense. Gliesians still hadn't actually landed on Earth, but the world was in negotiations for the first meeting between the two different species.

Or, at least, that's what was supposed to happen. The meet date had tentatively been assigned for 2145, when both humans and Gliesians would meet at a space station roughly half-way between the two planets. But the doctor had told Ophelia the full date of when she and Benny had gone to the Athens Astrosciences Department, including the year. No one said the year, unless you weren't in that year anymore.

"What year is it?" Ophelia asked, staring down at the doctor. "How long have I been under?"

The doctor didn't meet her eyes.

"A long time," he said. "You've been woken six other times, do you remember?"

Ophelia closed her eyes, trying to recall waking up here, in the cryo-med facility, before. Benny had been there, at least the first time, tear-stained and anxious. ... Why? Why had he been so upset? But there were other times. Other doctors. "You're not the doctor I saw last time," Ophelia said.

A smile cracked the doctor's old, weathered face, making the wrinkles on his cheeks and at his narrow eyes even more pronounced. "I'm not," he said gruffly. "I've got a bit more education and experience than the other fellow. One of the few advantages to getting old."

"You're a specialist?"

"I am." The doctor's smile wavered. "But let's go back to your memory. Do you recall now why you're here?"

"Benny and I snuck in to where they stored the Gliesian samples."

"The Gliesian ambassadors had sent over as many medical records and samples as possible," the doctor said. "The AAD had come up with a few tentative vaccinations—no cure. Not at that point."

Ophelia almost smiled in relief. The way the old doctor had said it sounded like there was a cure now. No more dead children, then.

But then Ophelia's mind replayed that night. Benny had been bragging to his new wife, showing off. The Gliesian anti-virus was beautiful—it glowed green and sparkled like emeralds. It had been very, very illegal for them to be there.

"But look at it," Benny had said, reaching up and taking the vial from its storage compartment.

"You'll get in trouble!" Ophelia had gasped.

Benny grinned wryly. "Nah, I won't. This is just a sample. We had something like it at our uni."

"This is what you were working on?" Ophelia leaned closer, peering through the crystal vial.

Benny nodded. "This is it. This should make it far safer for us to communicate with the Gliesians. Just think—this is what might open us up to a whole new universe! Our honeymoon's in Greece—maybe our tenth anniversary trip will be to Gliese!"

Ophelia laughed gaily, and Benny shushed her. They'd slipped away from the official tour, and it had only been Benny's ID code that had gotten them this far.

"This is better than magic," Benny said, looking down at the green vial in his hand.

"What happened?" the doctor asked softly, and it wasn't until that moment Ophelia realized she'd been telling the memory aloud.

"It was so stupid." Ophelia's voice was hollow. "We thought we heard someone coming, so Benny put the anti-virus back. And then we turned to leave, but he kissed me, and I kissed him, and the door opened, and I was so surprised that I stepped back." She took a deep breath. "I bumped into an open cabinet."

"You broke one of the Gliesian samples." There was no accusation in his voice, even though what he said was true.

She'd broken one of the samples. It shouldn't have been there. The Gliesian samples were on high-security lockdown—an alien virus had already killed millions, no one was willing to risk it happening again. But because of Benny's stupid credentials and because of a careless scientist who'd been working on the sample who left the compartment open and because of a kiss, and a stumble, and a crash...

"The vial broke."

Ophelia looked up at the doctor's eyes. "Is that why I'm here?" she asked. "I contracted some alien disease then?"

The doctor stared at his screen for several tense moments. He didn't lift his head when he finally said in a low voice, "Yes. And no. It wasn't the disease that killed you. It was the cure."

———

Ophelia was grateful that the doctor left her alone after this and gave her time to collect her thoughts. There were three people in the room when Ophelia had accidentally broken the vial: herself, Benny, and a young lab assistant named Andrea Zorbas, the girl who'd opened the door, startling Ophelia. Andrea had died instantly. Benny and Ophelia fell ill. Benny got better.

Ophelia had not.

Once it was clear that Ophelia was not recovering, she'd been put in the Greek cryo-med facilities. Benny transferred his study there, devoting his university career to finding a cure.

In 2144, a year before the Gliesian meeting at the space station, Benny found something that would kill the virus frozen inside Ophelia's body. The medication worked. The only problem was that it killed her, too. Or—

almost. They'd refrozen her, just before death claimed her. Trading eternal death for a temporary one.

Her weakness, her slow heartbeat, her disorientation, it all made sense. Ophelia wasn't sick. She was on the cusp of death. Real death. After being revived, Ophelia was quickly put back into the cryo-med facility. Countless doctors had worked on a new cure, and now, the new doctor had said, they had one.

The doctor cracked open the door, peering inside.

"You can come in," Ophelia said.

The doctor drew up a chair so that he could sit directly in Ophelia's line of sight. He seemed like a nice old man, someone who didn't deserve the burden of telling a girl she'd died once and was dying again.

"We think we have a cure this time," the doctor said. "You were never forgotten, not even after Benjamin Yuu's failed attempt to save your life with the original cure. We've been working with Gliesians—"

Ophelia gasped, and the doctor nodded, a frown of pity on his lips.

"How much time has passed?" Ophelia asked.

"It's now 2189. A Gliesian colony has been living on Earth for twenty years; a human colony has been on Gliese as well. Our species co-exist fairly peacefully now."

Ophelia's eyes widened. When she had been infected, contact had only just been made.

"By combining knowledge with the Gliesians, we've made several leaps in discovery. Some of our viruses have had massive negative effects on them as well. Actually you..."

"Yes?" Ophelia asked when the doctor didn't continue.

"Your case has been much studied, across both cultures. And it's been used in the peace negotiations. There was some conflict early on, some fear."

"And they used my body—?"

"Finding a cure for you was something both sides wanted—the humans, so that we'd be better equipped with anti-viruses; the Gliesians, so they could show their peaceful intent."

Ophelia found this difficult to comprehend. She was a symbol of peace? Her dead body negotiated life for two different species?

"But there's a cure now?" Ophelia asked softly. She wasn't sure she wanted it. So many decades had passed. All of her friends would be ancient. Her parents would be dead. And Benny—

Well, she didn't want to see him anyway.

He was responsible. He had killed her—not just by infecting her with a virus in a lab they never should have gone to, but also with a cure that had shut her body down, that had taken so many decades to recover from. A cure for the cure, leaving her with nothing.

"What was it like?" the doctor asked softly. "You looked so peaceful, just before I woke you."

Ophelia stared into his rheumy eyes. "It was like nothing," she said. "It was like existing in a state of nothing. I was not dreaming. I was not..."

"You were not what?" the doctor asked when Ophelia didn't answer.

"I was not," she said, looking straight through him. "I

wasn't. Right now, I am, but then, I wasn't. The thing that I was, was *not*."

She watched as his Adam's apple rose and lowered.

"I'm sorry," the doctor said.

"You didn't do this to me," Ophelia responded. Benny had. Stupid, foolish Benny. She shifted her focus sharply to the doctor, zeroing in on his eyes. "Please," she said. "Is there a cure now? Can I live again?"

The doctor adjusted the bags of fluid connected to the needles in Ophelia's arm. "Yes," the doctor said. "The cure has been tested. You'll stay here for observation, and then you'll enter a societal re-entry program."

Ophelia stared at him.

"The world has changed quite a bit since you went to sleep, O," the doctor said gently. "It will take some time to adjust. New tech. New sciences. And there's not just the Gliesians now, there's more."

The beeping heart-rate monitor spiked. "More?" Ophelia asked. What kind of world had she awoken to?

The doctor reached out to touch her, but he didn't, not quite. "More," he confirmed, a smile lingering on his lips. "I think you'll like it, O."

She wouldn't. She couldn't. Everything she'd ever loved had been taken away, all because of a stupid broken vial, in a lab her stupid new husband should have protected her from.

The doctor's smile faded.

"I have to go now," he said. "A nurse will be in to check on you soon, give you fluids and nutra-mix."

"Thank you," Ophelia mumbled. She had the strength

now to turn her head, and she did, looking not at the doctor as he left, but toward the wide open window to her right, the bright sunlight streaming in, highlighting the floating dust motes in the air.

———

As soon as the door zipped shut, the doctor's shoulders sagged. He appeared ten years older than his already advanced years. A Gliesian nurse tapped away at the screen at her station, but she looked up as the doctor walked slowly by.

"How is the patient?" she asked. It was hard for the doctor to understand what the nurse said; the Gliesian translator adjustors the aliens wore fizzled and crackled over time, and his old ears struggled to hear the English interpretation through the noise.

"The cure seems to be taking," he said. "Call me if there is any change."

The nurse nodded. "And doctor?"

The doctor glanced up.

"Thank you," the nurse said. "Your dedication to the patient has...well, you know what you've done. You brought our people together with the humans in an effort to find one cure. You have been a wonderful ambassador, developing the first Gliesian-human hospital. And what you've sacrificed for the patient—"

"It was nothing," the doctor said.

"Humans rarely live more than a hundred years, yes?" the Gliesian nurse asked. It was hard for them to understand this—Gliesians lived twice as long. "And you've spent nearly all of it trying to find a cure for this woman."

"She's not just a woman," Doctor Benjamin Yuu said, running his fingers through his thinning, white hair. "Not to me."

TWO

THE MOST PRECIOUS MEMORY

THERE ARE two types of people in the world—those who make memories and those who devour them.

Devon was one of the latter. He sat in the shadows of the alley, a dark man with dark thoughts who watched and waited. A girl with hair the color of sunset walked by, her red high heels tapping out a steady rhythm on the sidewalk that matched the swing of her hips and the swish of her hair. Devon barely noticed her; his eyes skimmed across the street and into the eyes of another man.

When their gaze met, a flash of understanding shot between them. Their world narrowed. There were no longer crowds of people on a busy city street, not even beautiful girls with hair the color of sunset. There were only the two of them, the buyer and the seller.

Something about the other man made Devon hesitate. A wave of déjà vu swept over him. He shook it off. One such as he were ever haunted by senseless déjà vu.

The other man had the stony face of one who is strong

enough to hide his pain. He crossed the street without checking the traffic and walked straight through the shadows to Devon.

"I've got a deal for you," he said without preamble.

Devon glanced up, fighting to keep the interest from his eyes. "I don't know what you mean," he said.

"Yes, you do. Make an offer."

Devon shrugged. "Perhaps," he said. "But I'll want to know exactly what you're selling." The man opened his mouth, but Devon held us his hand, his eyes darting back to the street. "Not here," he said. "Follow me."

Devon stood, steadying himself on the grimy wall he'd been leaning against. He took a deep breath. The other man watched his effort, but made no move to help him. He appeared disgusted by Devon's presence. Devon didn't care. Stumbling only a little, he led the other man down the alley.

The buildings towered over them, blocking the sun and what little warmth it provided. The alley twisted behind the walls, skirting the building and avoiding public streets. It was sprinkled with garbage cans and raggedy boxes and smears of filth.

"What's your name?" the man asked.

Devon rolled his eyes, but the other man, who was behind him, couldn't see. It was only those who still had their own memories that cared about names. There wasn't any point in remembering names. The memories of such useless trivia had hardly any taste at all.

"They call me Devon," he said and left it at that. There was no point explaining to this person who clung to his memories that the name wasn't really his own. He'd heard someone mention it in passing since the last time he'd awoken after a hit. That name was as good a one as any to give those who cared to know one.

"I'm Thomas."

Devon shrugged. He didn't care. It didn't matter.

When Devon stopped in front of the extraction hall, Thomas hesitated. Devon turned, not sure of what he could say to lure the other man inside. Before he could speak, however, Thomas strode past him, descended the steps, opened the door, and stepped into the poorly lit building. Devon followed.

The guard standing at the door narrowed his glance at Thomas, but Devon shook his head imperceptibly. He paid the fee for the use of the hall and led Thomas to a booth in the corner.

Around them people sat, each caught in their own trapped lives. Closest to the door, an older man lay across a table, sleeping off an extraction while the woman opposite him closed her eyes in transfixed bliss. Another man haggled over the price of his memories to a boy who looked much too young to be in the business. Across from the booth Devon and Thomas sat at was a young woman with a haunted face who pulled the extractor over her head so hastily that she accidentally yanked some hair from her skull. She did not seem to care.

"You said you wanted to make a deal," Devon said.

Thomas drug his gaze away from the girl at the other booth.

"Well?" Devon prompted when Thomas didn't speak.

"What would you pay," Thomas asked slowly, "for someone's most precious memory?"

Devon's eyes narrowed. This was not a common deal. Selling memories was—technically—illegal, but there were still enough people in the world desperate enough for money to sell, and enough people desperate enough for a fix to buy. Most of the time, though, people were willing to give up bad memories, like the pain of a broken bone as a child, or worthless memories, like the phone number of an ex. These memories could be broken up and devoured, but the satisfaction never lasted as long as a strong memory nor tasted as sweet as a precious one.

"Why would you want to give up such a memory?" Devon asked, unable to keep the wariness from his voice.

"Money."

Devon glanced at the gold watch on Thomas's wrist. Thomas pulled the sleeve of his immaculate linen shirt over it.

Something about the whole thing was suspicious. "I don't know..." Devon said, trailing off as he weighed his options. His ears rang. Being in the extraction hall made him monstrously starved.

Thomas leaned over the table, his elbow brushing up against the extractor, smearing grease on his sleeve. Thomas ignored it, not an easy feat considering how the extractor took up over half the table.

"Look," Thomas said, "I didn't say *a* precious memory. I said the *most* precious memory. Take it or leave it."

Devon's mouth watered. He'd never been offered such a deal. He knew of no one who had. Precious memories hardly ever came up for sale. They were too deep to be stolen, too valuable to be sold. They were virtually unattainable.

He had had one, a long time ago, before he had become what he was today. Once, Devon had been a normal boy. He was sure of it.

He just couldn't remember it.

Those who devour memories, who place more importance on the euphoria of the instant than the dull fulfillment of a lifetime, begin their downward spiral into addiction by eating their own memories. Devon had no recollection of the first memory he'd consumed—that of the taste of cold watermelon eaten on a warm day—but that was his first step to addiction.

He was just under twenty years old when he started. He was broke and alone, bored and tired. He had gone into an extraction hall not unlike this one, dark and sad, and he had set the extractor onto his head himself. It was simple enough. Think of the memory, push the red button on the front of the extractor, and wait for the pain to be over. In the end, the memory was nothing but a thin jet of liquid silver, but when he tipped it into his mouth, it exploded on his tongue. His senses burst in joy; his mind screamed in ecstasy; his body throbbed in pleasure.

It took him only three days to extract all his memories and eat them. After that, all that was left of his life was a mingling taste of joy on his lips. Then that, too, was gone. He became a buyer, his bloodshot hawk-eyes seeking out the desperation that led others to sell their memories.

But a most precious memory? This was something he'd

never tasted. Or, at least, it was something he couldn't remember ever tasting.

Thomas tapped his fingers on the table. "Deal or not?" he asked impatiently. Devon's eyes flitted over the man, staring into his eyes, trailing over the white outline at the edge of his lips, noting the way his jaw clenched and unclenched. Instinct told him this man would sell to him no matter what price he said.

"Fifty dollars."

"Fifty? You offer just fifty for a pure, perfect memory?"

Devon snorted. "How perfect could it be if you're willing to sell it?"

Thomas glared. "People sell their memories for many different reasons."

"Seventy-five."

"It's worth ten times that."

"I'm not the one desperate to sell."

"A thousand."

"A hundred." Devon held his breath. He was playing with fire. If he scared off this man, he wasn't sure where he'd find his next fix, and he needed it. Badly. But he only had a little over a couple hundred in his wallet, the left-overs of a commission for bringing some sellers to the extraction hall.

"Five hundred."

"Two."

"Three."

"Two." Devon tried to remember how much he actually had, but even though he'd looked in his wallet just moments before he'd first seen Thomas, it was all a blur.

The more one consumes memories , the harder it becomes to hold onto any.

Thomas seemed to be considering. "Fine. Two-hundred." He grimaced, as if selling at such a low price disgusted him.

Devon shifted his weight and pulled out his wallet, handing over most of the bills inside. Thomas pocketed them without counting them or even looking at them.

"Pleasure doing business with you, uh…"

"Tom," Thomas prompted when Devon's voice trailed off.

"Tom. 'Course. Pleasure doing business with you, Tom."

Devon watched Thomas with hungry eyes as he lifted the extractor from the table. Thomas met his eyes and held his gaze as he settled the heavy contraption onto his head. His hair stuck out under the rubber that cracked the base. Thomas's eyes did not leave Devon's until he pushed the red button and his eyes rolled back into his head.

Devon watched, counting the second methodically. The longer it took to extract the memory, the sweeter it could be, the longer the high would last. One. Two. Three. Four. Thomas's eyelids flickered over the white balls. Five. Six. Devon stared at the glass tube attached to the plastic hose that snaked down from the extractor. It was filling with silver liquid; it was already over a third full. Devon licked his lips. Had he had the money, he would have paid anything Thomas had asked.

Devon forgot how many second had passed, then forgot to count, then forgot he had been counting at all.

Thomas sighed and passed out, his head thumping on the table in front of him. Devon, who had been watching the spider crawl up the wall, jumped. He couldn't remember the man who lay sprawled across the table, but he recognized the extractor and the vial that was nearly overflowing with silver. Carefully, his hands shaking, he unscrewed the vial and held it in his hands. Other addicts glanced up from their booths and looked at him eagerly. Devon shifted in the booth, turning his back on them and shielding the vial from their gaze.

Bad memories are broken down, so the high lasts only seconds. Good memories are rare but taken whole, making the high last longer.

This memory was the strongest Devon had ever had. He felt his eyes vibrate in his skull, felt his body melt into blind stupor.

This was indeed a cherished memory, one that spanned years. Images sped through his mind, faster and faster. Flashes of childhood games played with a boy that looked oddly familiar were replaced with Christmases shared under the tree with the boy, and family vacations riding in the backseat with him, and the first day of school with the boy, older now, walking beside him. Devon realized that he'd just taken the memories of the other man's brother.

On some level of consciousness, Devon felt déjà vu.

The brothers played the same sports, joined the same clubs in school, helped each other with their homework. Devon smiled as the memories swept over him, absorbed into him. This was the fix he needed, the high he craved.

The images burst in his mind like flavor on the tongue. High school now. A new person was drawn into the memories. A girl with sunset hair, a girl who looked at the brother with the eyes of love. Double-dates and movies, prom and graduation.

Something, a wave of euphoria mixed with deep urgency, swept over Devon but was quickly drowned.

There was a name in the memories. James. The brother's name was James.

The girl with sunset hair flashed before Devon in his mind's eye, and the remembrance of love observed was replaced with the remembrance of real love. Thomas appeared in the memories again, laughing and happy. Thomas. The one who had sold the memories of his brother.

Something snapped within Devon, and with a shock that threw him out of his high, he realized that the brother in the memories was himself.

He was James. *He* was James. Thomas was *his* brother. The memories he was getting high off of were of himself.

He had never since his first high fought to keep a memory after he had consumed it. He fought now. If he let the memory fill his senses, if he let his mind devour it, it would be gone forever. And now, as flashes of his own life seen through his brother's eyes filled him, the man once called James and sometimes called Devon could think of nothing more than to hold onto the memories with everything he had.

Across the table, Thomas stirred.

With the slick-sweet taste of the memories still on his

lips, Thomas's brother clenched his eyes shut and concentrated on retaining the memories Thomas had sold him. There was sorrow within them now, starting with a bittersweet farewell as he left Thomas to go to college. He remembered his own voice in a conversation to his brother as he mentioned his first trip to the extraction hall. He remembered his brother's fear for him. The remembered the way he had looked on the last trip he'd taken home, and the way Thomas had tried to talk to him. He remembered the face of the girl with sunset hair after he'd broken up with her, then the way Thomas's heart had clenched with fear after he'd devoured his memories of her.

He remembered Thomas's memories of going into the city, tracking him down, watching him for days and seeing the blank look when their eyes met, day after day, until today, when he'd finally gotten the nerve to give him the only thing he had to save him.

He remembered, and he would not let himself forget. Not again. Not after seeing it through his brother's fading memories.

Thomas groaned and lifted his head, his neck straining under the unaccustomed weight of the extractor.

"Tom?"

Thomas pulled the extractor off and set it on the table. "Where am I?"

"In an extraction hall."

Thomas blinked in surprise. He glanced down, rubbing a smear of grease on his otherwise pristine shirt. He took a deep breath, then looked back up.

"Who are you?" he asked.

"I'm James," the man who had once forgotten his own name said.

For one full second, recognition flashed in Thomas's eyes. Then nothing.

It had simply been déjà vu.

THREE

THE GIRL & THE MACHINE

"OH, MY GOSH, IT'S YOU!" A pretty girl dropped to her knees in front of Franklin. She had honey-colored eyes that seemed to glow next to her dark skin and bright smile. He stared at her, his mouth opening slightly in shock.

"I'm sorry—" he started.

"No, no, don't be, I'm just so excited!" The girl slid off her knees, sitting down fully in the grass beside him. "I'm Heather." She stuck her hand out. He looked at it. "Heather Gardner-Wells," she added, as if that made a difference.

Franklin hesitantly shook her hand, barely touching her fingers, then dropped it. Heather scooted closer.

Below them, a car blared its horn on Elm Street. Dealey Plaza wasn't an ideal place for a study session, but Franklin loved it. He loved the history of the place. It felt momentous, just being there.

"I thought I might see you here," the girl said eagerly. "I mean, you told me not to track you down, and of course I *tried*, but I'd be lying if I didn't say I figured that, of all the places in Texas you'd be, it'd be here."

"I'm sorry," Franklin repeated. "But I really don't know you. I'm afraid you've got me mixed up with someone—"

Heather straightened her back and met Franklin's gaze with twinkling eyes. "You're Franklin Poteat," she said triumphantly, "and you were born in North Carolina, but you moved in with your gram here in Fort Worth soon after you hit puberty because she had Alzheimer's and you had, well..." She paused. "You know."

Franklin grew very, very still.

"Your...condition...means that you need to have someone not too concerned when you disappear for a bit, and besides, you thought you could help your gram out. And it worked for a bit, but then she died." Heather gasped and covered her mouth with her hands. "I'm sorry!" she exclaimed. "I didn't mean to say it so bluntly. But anyway, you were old enough to, er, travel as you please after that, you had better control, and..." She looked down. "I...uh. I'm going to stop talking now. Sorry."

Franklin stared at her, his mouth slightly open in shock.

"We should go somewhere more private," he said.

Heather looked up, her eyes bright and eager.

"Where someone else can't hear us," Franklin continued.

Heather leapt to her feet. Franklin was slower as he gathered his books and carefully put them away in his leather knapsack. His hands were shaking. *How did she know?* His brain tried to figure out how she could possibly know his secret...and how he could possibly have known her. She stood there, bubbly and excited, as if all of this was perfectly normal.

She led him to the library—not to the books, but to the little greenhouse off to the left of it. It was just a decorative thing, really more like a glass-enclosed gazebo with far too many ferns. It had been intended as a quiet place to study, but a greenhouse in Texas was never a good place to study. It was always empty.

The air was stiflingly hot and stuffy, but Franklin shut the door anyway.

For a moment, he stared out the dirty glass, trying to find the right words to say, hoping that when he turned around Heather wouldn't be there.

"You're probably wondering how I know you," Heather stated.

Franklin turned to face her. Gone was the effervescent excitement. Heather looked as somber as he felt, and there was worry—or fear?—in her eyes now.

"It's not every day that someone comes up to me and says, 'hey, I know your deepest, darkest secret.'"

Heather laughed, but there was no amusement in the sound. "I suppose it's not every day someone meets a time traveler."

To have it stated like that, so simply and in such a matter-of-fact voice, threw Franklin off. The only people he'd ever tried to tell about his condition were his parents (who didn't believe him) and his gram (who had, but couldn't do anything about it).

"How do you know that?" Franklin asked, glaring at her. "Have we met in the past?"

Heather smiled slowly, but again there was no mirth in her look, not like before. She shook her head. "We didn't meet in the past," she said. She stepped closer to him, and her hands shook as she reached for his cheek, her fingers barely brushing along the edge of his jaw.

"Then how did we meet?" Franklin asked. "How do you know so much about me?"

Heather's eyes did not leave Franklin's. "We met in your future."

Franklin jerked back. That was...impossible. He didn't pretend to be an expert in his own ability to travel through time, but he was the only person he knew who could actually do what he did. He had started travelling through time by accident. When he got older, he was able to gain a certain level of control over his ability, but even so he had limits. He'd never traveled forward into the future, and he had never traveled past his own time-line. The most back he could go was the day he was born, and no matter how much he tried, he could never go into tomorrow—he always landed in today. And he *had* tried—many times. He had tried for greed, in an effort to learn the winning lottery ticket numbers. He had tried for curiosity, to find out his own future, and the world's. But nothing he ever did worked. His future was as cloudy as everyone else's; only his own past was clearer.

And yet... Here was this girl who knew his secret. Who knew him. And as much as he did not want to believe her, he couldn't see any other way she could know about his ability.

As the realization that Heather was speaking the truth dawned on him, Heather started to smile. It was a ferocious smile, the same kind of smile a predator has when it first sees its prey.

"I have known you for a very long time," Heather said. "More than six years. And throughout that time, I have been waiting for this day."

"And what happens today?" Franklin asked, apprehension seizing him.

"Today's the day when everything changes," Heather said. "Today's the day we change the world."

———

"This is so weird," Franklin said. He pushed his small suitcase back and forth on its wheels, focusing on the whisper of the sound of the plastic wheels sliding along the cold tile floor. He ignored the rush of people around him. Heather had arrived at the airport before him. She seemed to have no trouble believing that he would absolutely follow her here. When she had left him at the greenhouse, after telling him everything, she had just handed him a plane ticket and walked away. He'd considered tossing it. But in the end, his curiosity had won out. He had no idea why he trusted this girl. He couldn't explain it. But she seemed familiar to him. She felt like an old friend.

She felt like someone he could trust.

Still: "It's just *so* strange," he repeated.

"Weirder than the ability to time travel?" Heather asked with a smirk.

For Franklin, yes. Having a girl approach him while studying on a random Tuesday afternoon and telling him his entire life story and informing him casually that he was going to change the world today was definitely a new experience. Time travel was tame in comparison. Time travel to him was nothing more than an afternoon adventure. He used travel to steal extra naps during study sessions or to get away from the pressures of college. Very, very occasionally he actually used it to help him be a better history major. He was restricted to his own timeline, but he was able to enhance his report on terrorism by actually watching 9/11 happen in real time. He had won an award for his portrayal of the devastation of Hurricane Katrina from the history department, and no one had ever known that his sources were all firsthand.

For everyone else on earth, time travel was surely an anomaly. He could see why so many people would find it fascinating, including Heather. He'd asked her dozens of times, and she confirmed every single time: She was not a traveler, not like him. She had met him in high school, but when she had met him, he was 38 years old. He wasn't a history professor, as he always supposed he would be, which was why he was spending so much money getting that degree. Instead, he was the world's only time traveler. Not many people knew, but some did. Important people. He was wealthy. He was powerful.

And he needed Heather's help. In the future.

"So, I came to your past, but I was in my future," Franklin said slowly.

"Yes," Heather said. "I was in high school, it was just after my prom, and I was sincerely freaked out." She laughed. "I'm not even sure how you knew it was me. I looked very different then." She touched her dark hair pulled into a neat bun. "Anyway, you found me. You were really concerned about it all. We were both desperately worried that you were going to create a paradox, and it would ruin everything. I think that's why you went so far back into my past. I was just old enough to understand what you were saying, but not old enough to make a difference."

"And now you are?"

Heather checked the flight boards. Their flight was running ten minutes late, and the flight attendant at the desk was loudly confirming to a group of businessmen that the delay was really only ten minutes, and they would probably be able to make the time up in the air.

"I am young," Heather conceded. "Let's just say that meeting you changed my life. I was always studious, but you gave me a purpose."

Franklin looked down at his ticket again. Massachusetts. Heather was about his age, but she was in a far more advanced program of study than just a general history degree like him. She was one of the top students at MIT. Heather was working directly with a famous theoretical engineer professor, and she had her own laboratory space.

"So what did future-me tell you to do?" Franklin said.

Heather averted her gaze. "I'm not supposed to tell you everything," she said. "I know it's difficult, but you're going to have to trust me."

Franklin's grip on his suitcase's handle tightened. He didn't like the unknown. He always wanted to know exactly what was occurring around him. There were times in the past when he spied on himself just to get a different perspective on what had happened at certain moments in his life. He looked around the crowd at the airport now, trying to see some future version of himself spying on this moment. One of the businessmen caught his eyes. A tall white man with short brown hair and dark hazel eyes. The exact same shade of eye color as he himself had. Franklin's gaze intensified as he tried to figure out if this businessman was actually him, from the future, watching.

The businessman looked away.

Franklin pressed Heather for more details, but she refused to answer. "I'll tell you more when I can show you what I have in the lab," Heather said.

Franklin tried to assess what this meant. After Heather had met the future version of himself after her prom, she had dedicated all of her time and energy in doing...something...for him. Or, rather, for his future self. Something that his future self needed. Something that, as Heather had said, changed the world.

The flight attendants opened the gate and started the boarding process. The businessmen were among the first to push their way to the front of the first-class lane. The man with hazel eyes who Franklin thought might be himself glared at the woman with a small baby who neatly maneuvered her stroller around the clusters of businessman to the front of the line.

Franklin barely paid any attention as he handed his pass over to the flight attendant and she scanned him in. He followed Heather like an automaton, blithely accepting the aisle seat she offered him as she slipped into the window seat.

The thing was, this all felt...momentous. The fact that he had somehow figured out how to travel into the future, he had chosen Heather as one of the first points of contact to make...that all meant that she was important. That they were important together. That what they were going to do would be something that would really make a difference.

Change the world, like Heather said.

The first time Franklin had ever used his ability, he was eight years old. It had been a complete accident. He had broken a toy he had just received at his birthday party the previous day. He clutched the rubber wheel of the brand-new remote controlled car in his hands, and he had wished with all his might that he could go back and stop himself from attempting to drive the car over a makeshift ramp into a pile of rocks. Somewhere in that passionate desire, his ability to travel through time had been triggered. He blinked backwards to ten minutes prior. He hadn't been able to change anything; he had been too shocked. He had just watched the destruction of the remote controlled car all over again, then blinked and was back in his own timeline.

He'd experimented since then and gotten better at his

abilities, but he'd never done anything...remarkable. He'd never done something that would make a difference.

The flight attendants walked up and down the aisle of the plane, checking overhead compartments and that everybody was wearing a seatbelt. They started their spiel about safety as the plane taxied out onto the runway.

Franklin leaned over to Heather. "So the stuff that we're doing... It's really important, isn't it?"

"Why does that seem so shocking to you?" Heather asked sincerely. "You have the ability to literally travel in time. You could do... You *will* do so much good for the world. Is that really such a surprise to you?"

Franklin could not meet the fire and Heather's eyes. The truth of the matter was, it was a surprise to him. His abilities to travel through the time were limited, true, but he had never really thought about how he could use them for anyone but himself.

"I don't think I'm quite the person that you met when you were in high school yet," Franklin said.

Heather touched the back of Franklin's hand and didn't speak until he met her eyes again. "You are exactly the person that I met when I was in high school," she said. "I have no doubt of that."

———

Massachusetts was considerably colder than Texas had been, made more so by the biting wind. Franklin was rather glad that Heather was taking him directly to MIT and her lab there.

He had expected the lab to be a part of MIT, but instead Heather drove them straight by the main campus, down several back alleys, and into the country. The lab itself was at the end of a narrow dirt road in the middle of the field. Franklin wondered if creepy horror movie music would start playing in the background.

Heather glanced at him and laughed. "Trust me, it's better on the inside."

And she wasn't lying. After scanning her thumbprint on a biometric lock, tapping in a nine digit code on a numerical pad, and fitting a key into a slot by the door, Heather let Franklin inside. "Welcome home!" Heather said.

It seemed clear that Heather practically lived here in the lab. Near the front, there was a slightly open door through which Franklin could see a made-up bed—not a cot but an actual bed—and the clutter of a lived-in apartment. The lab itself was immaculate. Despite the fact that the outside of it had looked rather worn down, made of cement blocks with no windows and overgrown grass around the edges, the inside of the laboratory was gleaming steel and the harsh scent of antiseptic.

"This is it," Heather said taking Franklin by the hand and dragging him across the laboratory toward a large metal object that took up most of the room. A line of computers stood against the wall, flashing code and incomprehensible numbers Franklin didn't understand. Not that he understood the machine in the middle of the room, either. There was a platform to the left with what looked like a glass cylinder that could wrap around it, much like the little tubes that drive-through banks used to get money to the tellers. Attached to it was another tube, but this one was made entirely of metal with a small glass pane near the top. Franklin stood in front of it looking into the glass pane. The metal tube was about the same size as he was, and the glass plate was even with his face. Behind the contraption was a jumble of metal boxes, exposed circuit boards, and bundles of wires and coiled tubing illuminated by blinking LED lights.

"Forgive the mess," Heather said.

"What is this?" Franklin asked, staring at up at the gleaming metal.

"The time machine," Heather said.

Franklin stared at her as if waiting for her to laugh again and tell him this was all a joke. As a time traveler, he probably shouldn't think that such a machine was impossible but... But it was.

"This is what I've been working on, pretty much my entire time here," Heather said. Her voice was very serious. "In fact, this is really what I've been working on since I met you. I've always been fascinated with this kind of technology, I've always felt like it was possible, but I never dared to actually work on it. Why would anyone waste their time working on a time machine? I knew the theory and the science, but it was impossible right? And then you. You, from the future. And somehow just knowing that it was actually possible was enough for me to make it actually happen."

"So...does it work?" Franklin asked, unable to take his

eyes away from the gigantic machine that hummed with life.

Heather walked around the machine, lovingly touching the metal, stroking it as she would stroke a lover's skin. "Theoretically, yes. We've done all the tests and studies that we could possibly do. But we cannot make it actually work." She looked up at him. "Not without you."

"Me?"

Heather nodded. "We need you—or more precisely, we need your genetics."

Franklin looked down at his hands, then back up to Heather.

"There's something in your blood, in your DNA, that gives you the ability to travel. A mutation."

"Like the X-Men?"

Heather laughed, but again Franklin noticed there was no humor in the sound. "Sort of," she said. "Anyway, without this mutation, the time machine won't work. We need you to make it work."

"How?"

"It's very simple," Heather said. "What happens is, you step into the machine, we program it for whatever time and place you want, the machine reads your genetic code, and then it uses your own genetic mutation to send you exactly where you want to go—past or future."

Franklin stared at the machine, trying to think of all the things that he could do with it. Time travel could be rather mundane when one is limited to your own timeline. With a machine like this, he could see the dinosaurs. He could see whatever happened to humanity a hundred years —a thousand years—several millennia from now.

"Yes, hello?" Heather said. Franklin looked up and realized she was using her cell phone. "One large." She glanced up at Franklin. "You like pepperoni?" Franklin nodded. "Large pepperoni," Heather said into the phone. She hung up. "We have to eat," she said to Franklin. "It's going to be a long night."

———

They sat at the base of the machine on either side of the greasy pizza box, using napkins as plates. The pizza came from some local place rather than a chain, but the only difference between it and any other pizza he could get was that the crust was far too big and lumpy.

Franklin sat with the machine behind him. It felt as if it loomed over him, watching his every move. He ate the pizza nervously.

"Most people can't travel through time at all," Heather said. "Obviously. But since you can go to the past, there's really no reason why you can't also go into the future."

"I just assumed it'd make a paradox or something," Franklin said weakly.

"A paradox?"

"Like, if I went forward in time, I'd break the universe." He felt rather stupid in front of this girl genius. He should have learned more about his own condition, about the science behind it. He felt like a cancer victim who had never bothered to learn about germs.

Heather dropped her half-eaten slice back in the box and scooted closer to Franklin. "It doesn't work like that. You've tried to go forward in time, right? And it never worked?"

Franklin nodded in agreement.

"It's like this." Heather pulled Franklin up and led him to a gurney at the back of the lab. She pushed him onto the wheeled table and started to roll it forward. "For everyone else on Earth, we can only move through time in one direction." She pushed the gurney forward. "We have no control over how fast we're going, or that we can only move forward. But you do." She tapped his knee, and Franklin dropped his foot to the slick, tiled floor, then used the traction of his sneaker to push back against Heather, making the wheels of the gurney go backwards. "But you're still limited. You have a block of some sort, something that's preventing you from moving more than backwards and forwards within your own previously-lived timeline. With the machine, we unblock the restrictions you currently have, and you're free to go anywhere in time that you like." She pushed him off the gurney, and Franklin was free to move as he wanted to.

He still didn't fully understand what the machine would do to him or how it would work, but Heather plopped back down in front of the pizza, satisfied she had fully explained herself.

"What makes a person like you want to spend her life working on a machine like this?" Franklin asked, sitting back down. He didn't eat any more. His stomach was upset; his nerves were on edge.

"You made a lasting impression." She stared at him with clear, sincere eyes. Then she shrugged. "I've always been sort of nerdy, anyway," Heather said dismissively.

To be honest, it surprised Franklin. Heather wasn't super-model gorgeous, but she was hot enough. Her dark skin was smooth, and her hair had been relaxed and twirled up into a cute bun. Heather had a little bit of a hot-librarian-thing going for her. She wasn't exactly slender, but she had an everyday-girl charm about her that Franklin found attractive.

She didn't look like a nerd. Like a genius.

Gooey cheese slid down her pizza, landing with a greasy plop on the napkin. Heather looked down at it as if surprised she was still eating.

"I wasn't always the way I am now," she said softly. "High school was hell. I was a 'late bloomer,' so to say. I didn't get boobs until I was a junior. I wasn't into the same things other girls my age were. Didn't care about make-up or hair products. Never interested in boys." She glanced up. "I'm not interested in girls, either," she said somewhat defensively. "I have always only been interested in science. But try defining asexuality to a bunch of horny teenagers in high school. Try explaining to them that you really, sincerely would rather study and learn about physics and genetics than put on cheap glitter and go to a party. It doesn't really work out well, let me tell you."

"I'm sorry," Franklin said.

Something like steel edged the look in Heather's eyes. "I've changed some since then," Heather said. "I had to."

She tossed her head toward the light gleaming from the

machine. She wore a little makeup—just a thin outline of turquoise around her eyes and a burgundy shade of lipstick —and she'd obviously done her hair for both looks and practicality. For the first time, however, Franklin realized that Heather had carefully manufactured her appearance not so much to look good, but the same way a warrior might wear armor. Her neat, slightly preppy clothes, the way she did her face—it was all a front, a disguise so people would leave her alone and let her do what she wanted. It was easier for her to cave to the norms of society in her appearance than to argue that she didn't care about it at all.

"My senior year, I really figured things out," Heather said, still not looking at Franklin. "I got the right clothes, the right look. I started blending in with the popular kids. I got invited to parties, but it wasn't until my prom that I actually went to any."

The corner of Franklin's mouth tilted up in a smile. "And then future-me crashed that party, right?" he asked, remembering the way Heather had described their meeting.

She nodded.

"And that changed everything." She paused for a long time. "Anyway, what about you? What was it like, growing up with this ability to go through time?"

"Not as glamorous as you may think," Franklin said. "I could never go anywhere I really wanted to go."

Heather smiled. "Like to witness the big events of history."

"Exactly!" Franklin's face lit up. "That's why I'm a history major, I guess. I'm fascinated with the past, because it always seems just at the tips of my fingers. Honestly, I'm more excited about using the time machine to go into the past beyond my own timeline than into the future."

"Where would you go first?" Heather asked.

"Um..." Franklin pondered the question. He'd of course thought about it before. As a kid, he'd wanted nothing more than to see an actual T-Rex. But now, he probably most wanted to see...

"The JFK shooting?" Heather answered for him.

"How'd you know?"

"I told you, I know you!" Heather crowed. "How did you think I found you this morning, studying at the grassy knoll?"

Had it really only been this morning that Heather had plopped down into his life?

"I wasn't on the grassy knoll," Franklin said. "But I guess it is kind of a creepy place to hang out."

"You are a proper Dallas boy after all," Heather added.

Franklin grinned sheepishly. Maybe it was weird that he most wanted to see another man die, but it was a topic that had always fascinated him. The shooter on the hill, the conspiracy theories, the end of an era. He wanted to witness it all.

"And then just really momentous moments and people in history. D-Day. Alexander the Great. A slave auction. Hell, it'd be cool to go back far enough to meet Jesus, just to confirm that he was really there."

"You're not interested in the future at all?"

"One of the first things I'd do is go forward and find out the winning numbers to the biggest lotto in the country, that's for sure," Franklin said immediately. "And I'd do enough to make sure that I was never poor. Maybe get into politics. Buy the best houses. There's this dick in my Reformation History class—I may try to screw with him a little."

Heather grew silent, watching him. Finally she said, "Have you ever done that before, screwed with people's pasts?"

"Well, yeah," Franklin said. "Wouldn't you? You have the ability to change the past—wouldn't you do it to get revenge on the assholes in your life?"

"Such as?"

"There was this one kid—Jeremy—in my high school. He was always trying to one-up everyone. Freaking valedictorian, every teacher loved him, he was even star of the football team. Total cliché, total 'good guy' who never did anything wrong."

"What'd you do to him?" Heather asked quietly.

Franklin shrugged. "I just...I went back in time and messed up his college applications. You should have seen his face when everyone else started getting accepted to schools, and he didn't." He shrugged again. "It didn't matter anyway; the counselors at school made sure he got a late entry into one of his back-ups."

Heather's eyes searched his. "If someone had messed with my MIT application, we wouldn't be here now."

"Look, I know it was a jerk thing to do. But Jeremy totally deserved to be taken down a peg, that guy had it far too easy in life."

Heather didn't say anything.

"Okay, fine, I know I've been kind of an asshole about this whole ability in the past. It didn't take me long to realize that I could basically do anything without consequences."

Heather waited for him to continue.

"So, yeah, maybe I did some dick things. I shouldn't have messed up Jeremy's college apps. I...I stole, too. I'm not proud of it, but I did. When the latest games would sell out, I'd just go back in time to when the shipment arrived at the store, steal one, and then pop back into the present. It was easy. It didn't hurt anyone."

She just watched him. It was like her silence forced him into a confession.

"You can't sit there and tell me that you wouldn't do the same sort of thing," Franklin said defensively. "You don't know what it's like, having this power and knowing you can do whatever you want."

"Well, as long as you didn't hurt anyone," she said in an even monotone.

Franklin paused. That wasn't really true, was it? He'd tried to ruin Jeremy's life. And then...

"I wasn't a good person, okay?" Franklin said, looking down. "I...I wasn't one of the cool guys, okay? I was always shy and quiet, and I was bullied a lot. Going back in time was a way to cope. I could solve my problems in the past, and then come into the future. If I hadn't been able to do that, shit, I would have no confidence right now."

"What do you mean?" Heather asked, her voice still without inflection.

"You said you learned how to be hot, got invited to

parties and stuff, right? I learned by going back in the past, doing things over. It gave me confidence. I'd go back in time and crash parties. There were no consequences in the past, yeah? I could do what I wanted. No one would ever catch me. I started going to parties a couple of towns over, meeting girls I never would have met before. Drunk girls do a lot to boost a nerdy guy's confidence, let me tell you."

Franklin could tell Heather was judging him, and it made him feel as if he had to prove that he was right. "Okay, so, look. I was at this one party. It was huge. There were dozens of people there, maybe a hundred. My own prom and the party after had been...god, it was a disaster. Total swing and a miss. But at this party, I didn't know anyone, not really. And if I made a complete fool of myself, I could just disappear into the present, yeah? So there was this one girl. Total hottie. She was quiet, like me, and by herself. By the pool. So...no consequences, right? I talked to her. She was nice. Maybe a little drunk, but who cares? I took her to the pool house, and we did it. She was reluctant, but it didn't matter. Losing my v-card like that; shit, the next day at school, I walked like a king. And the other guys could see it, too. Things changed for me."

Heather waited until Franklin met her eyes. "So you raped her?"

Franklin's face registered shock. "Rape? I wouldn't call it rape! It's not like I ambushed her and ripped her clothes off and forced her."

"You said she was reluctant."

"Yeah, well, she had obviously been a virgin, too."

"Did she say yes?"

"She didn't say no."

"Stop, uh-huh, I want you to think about this. You walked into the party looking to get laid. You knew you would have no consequences for whatever you did there. You met a girl, alone, and took her to a private place. I want you to really think about that night. Did you rape her?"

Franklin wasn't sure why Heather was so stuck on that point. What did it matter? It was in the past... All he remembered of that night was the warmth of her body, the thrill of the conquest. It had been a conquest. A battle to overcome. Because...she had fought. Weakly, he thought, but maybe she'd been tired or drunk. The word "no," had never actually been said, but then again, he hadn't been listening, had he? He had barely even looked at her. Because when he did, when he looked down at her terror-stricken face and deadened eyes...no. He had just looked away. Easier to not look, to just feel. If she hadn't wanted it, if she hadn't wanted him, she should have said no. She should have fought harder. It wasn't rape. Rape was done by criminals who jumped from dark shadows. Rape was violent. It had just been sex. He had wanted it.

But he had never really checked to make sure she had.

"Okay, fine, I'm no saint," Franklin said, his voice rising. He found he couldn't meet Heather's eyes. "Maybe that played out badly."

She didn't answer him. The words hung between them. He could tell that she was disappointed in him, and it upset him in a way he hadn't expected. When Heather described meeting the future version of him, it was noble.

A man using his abilities for good, not just to get laid by a girl he didn't even know.

"Were there other girls?" Heather asked. "Other girls who didn't know you would have 'no consequences' for whatever you did?"

Franklin looked away. There had been. A dozen or more. He had learned—after trial and error—that the best method for him was to find the quiet girls, the ones who didn't really seem to belong to the parties, the ones who followed him to the private places, the upstairs rooms or the dark backyards. He had learned to not look at them after he started. He had learned not to say much, to go straight to the action. And he had learned to disappear quickly after he finished, to leave them on the bed or in the damp grass, to walk out of sight and silently slip back to his own time. He had learned, he realized, to never even think the word "rape," that it was only the word that made it true to him.

"I'm not that kind of guy anymore," Franklin said quietly. He didn't need to be. Being with those girls had given him the confidence he needed to be more outgoing, to join a frat, to risk meeting girls in his own timeline, to not fear rejection.

His abilities had turned him into the man he was now —confident, courageous, sure of himself and his potential.

"I haven't been the best guy I could be, I guess," Franklin said. "Maybe I did use my powers greedily. But you met the future version of me. Clearly I can change. Clearly *this* is the point where I stop using my ability to benefit just myself and really try to do things that are better for other people."

Heather shot him a small smile. "I am sure that will be the outcome," she said. She slapped her knees and stood up. "Are you ready to try?"

Franklin stared at her. "Tonight?"

Heather nodded. "Why not? It won't take long to run just a simple trial."

Franklin wanted to say no, but there was really no reason to. "What will it do?" he asked. The steel and chrome and wires and glass seemed heartless and menacing.

Heather took him by the hand and led him to the metal tube. Pushing a button, it opened with a hydraulic hiss. "You get in here," she said. "The machine will read your genetic code—it will have to take a small sample of blood, but it won't hurt—and it will use that to fuel the machine. Then you get out, stand on the platform, and go anywhere in time you want to go."

"Just like that?"

"Just like that."

She pushed him gently toward the open tube. He stepped inside—it fit him perfectly, like a custom-made coffin. Heather leaned on her tip-toes, her breasts pressing into his chest as she pulled down a set of tubes from the top of the metal enclosure. At one end was a long needle.

"Take your shirt off," she said matter-of-factly.

"I—really?"

"Really."

Franklin pulled his t-shirt off and dropped it at Heather's feet.

"Okay, so this part may actually hurt just a little," Heather said, holding the needle. "You should maybe shut your eyes."

"Where are you putting that thing?" Franklin said, staring at the long, gleaming shaft of metal.

"Just trust me. It won't hurt that much. And you're going to thank me after."

Something about those words...those words sounded familiar.

But he did it. He shut his eyes and turned away. In a moment, a hard, cold feeling rushed into his body, and he cried out in pain.

"Holy *shit,*" he screamed. "What was that?" He looked down at the trickle of blood sliding down his chest, at the tubing connected directly to his heart. "Ohmygod, did you stick that thing in my *heart*? Holy shit, holy shit!"

"Calm down," Heather said, pressing her hands into his bare chest. "Calm down. It's not that big of a deal."

"There is a *needle* in my *heart!*"

"You're fine," Heather said.

"You said this was going to be simple!"

She shrugged. "I lied."

A thin line of red pulsed out of one end of the tube— his blood. Franklin shivered. Another line of something almost silvery with shimmering blue specks was pumping in through the tube, filling his heart with cold.

"What are you doing to me?" His hands went instinctively to the tube.

Heather glanced at him. "Pull that out, and you may go into cardiac arrest," she said. When he didn't move his hands, she added, "You could die."

"You said this was simple; that it wouldn't hurt!"

The look on her face dismissed his words completely. "You told me that once as well." Franklin stared at her, unable to understand her words. "So, anyway," Heather continued in her cool, scientific voice, "your blood is currently being scanned and the machine is fueling up."

"Thank goodness; then I can get out of here, right?"

Heather smiled. "This liquid, here"—she tapped the other tube, the silvery-and-blue one—"is pumping cryostasis liquid into you."

"Cryo-what?"

"Cryostasis liquid. It will actually slow down time for you. You won't need to eat or sleep or use the bathroom. Once I shut this door, you'll be living in your own personal loop of time, basically. Five years will feel like five seconds."

"What?" Franklin asked, but the word came out slow. *Whhuuuuuuuuuuuut?*

Heather nodded to herself and checked something on a chart by the door. "It's starting to hit your system, good. Before I close the door—before I complete the process—I want you to know that I couldn't have done any of this without you."

Franklin stared at her.

"'Just trust me. It won't hurt that much. And you're going to thank me after.'" She said the words in a cruel, mocking tone. "I will never forget when you said those words to me. You said them over me, while you were over my body, while your voice overrode my own. You didn't even recognize me today, you asshole. And today, you *bragged* about what you did to me? That raping me made you the man you are?" She glared at him, derisiveness seeping from her body. "I was just learning how to be normal, and you yanked that away, just like you yanked my clothes off me."

Horror filled Franklin's chest, a hot sort of feeling drowned quickly out by the cold pumping through his body.

"You had no idea who I was. You had no idea what I was capable of. It didn't take me that long to track you down. I didn't want to believe that you had this impossible ability, but I watched you. You never noticed me. You never notice anyone but yourself. I watched what you did, and I realized how you could get away with it all."

Heather put her hands on the door to the little metal coffin. Franklin struggled to move, to stop her from closing him in, but he couldn't. She moved so *fast*, and his body was so, so *slow*.

Before she closed the door, she paused, turning to face him. "At least I've found a way to make your power useful." She snorted. "You thought you were some hero in the future, didn't you? You really bought that I met future-you at that party. Nope. Just past-you. Just-asshole you. That's who I met. There *is* no future-you. *This* is your future. All you are now is a battery. A battery to fuel *my* machine, to let *me* travel wherever I want, in the past, in the future—anywhere. And I'm not going to be like you. I'm going to be the hero you never could be."

She slammed the door shut. The hydraulics hissed, and a wisp of smoke or steam or something clouded the glass faceplate. When it cleared, Heather's face filled Franklin's vision.

"You took a lot away from me that night," she said, loudly enough for him to hear her through the glass. "But all I'm going to take from you now is your time."

She flicked a switch, and a metal screen slid down over the faceplate.

Franklin was trapped in the darkness with nothing but time.

FOUR

LAG

"WHERE AM I?" Kimiko asked, her voice raw from disuse. She struggled to stand.

"Careful now." A man she didn't recognize rushed forward. He wore a white lab coat over his street clothes. Across the top right of the coat the logo for Teleportation Services shone, a bright blue *TPS* circled in orange. Where was she? This man spoke English with an American accent, but that meant little at a teleportation station.

"Did I—?" Kimiko looked around as the young man helped her stand. Behind her was a teleportation platform, still flickering with remnants of energy.

"Is this your first teleport?" the attendant asked.

Kimiko shook her head. She teleported almost weekly; how else could she be one of the top freelance news reporters? People relied on her, personally, to provide the truth.

The teleportation attendant scanned her in, then

checked her luggage box. "Arriving in Tokyo from London," he said. "Did you enjoy London?"

Kimiko shook her head, still confused. Had she enjoyed London? She didn't remember London.

The attendant looked up, his eyes narrowing as he examined Kimiko more carefully. "Are you okay, Ms. Murasaki?"

"No, and don't touch me," she muttered in Japanese, but she kept her voice low, just in case the attendant understood the language. She glanced at his name tag. Todd. *Todd.* He looked like a Todd.

Todd glanced at his scanner. "Can you tell me how long you were in London, Ms. Murasaki?"

Kimiko froze. She couldn't. Without meeting Todd's eyes, she moved closer to her luggage box.

"What is your earliest memory?" Todd asked, his voice pitching another note higher.

Kimiko hid her emotion behind her sweep of dark hair. Her earliest memory? June 2. Her eyes flicked to the row of world clocks lined behind the teleportation platform. June 17. She was missing more than two weeks from her mind.

"Ma'am, Ms. Murasaki, I think you might be experiencing something called time-lag. It's a rare occurrence that happens in less than one percent of teleportation travelers, but it would require some medical attention that we would be happy to administer to you at this time—"

Kimiko whirled around to face the attendant. He paused in his tapping on the scanner—probably calling for a more senior officer to come help out. "I'm fine," she said. "I just got...disorientated."

"You should go to our medical bay," Todd said. "We have a time-lag research facility in-house."

Kimiko picked at the shoulders of the pale green thin jumpsuit—the teleportation-safe material was the only thing allowed to touch the skin during a trip. "At least let me change first," she said, pushing a button on her luggage box and extending a handle.

Todd hesitated, but Kimiko had been at this station enough to know what to do. She headed toward the hallway and the changing room. "I'll be waiting, ma'am; we really should check whether or not you have time-lag. It's for your own well being."

Kimiko waved him off without looking back as the door to the changing room opened. She stepped into the cubicle, but rather than opening her luggage box, she leaned over the sink, staring at herself in the mirror.

Two weeks. She was missing two weeks.

What the hell had happened?

Kimiko had travelled enough to have gotten time-lag before, but that had only lost her one day. This was...far worse. She tried to remember what the medical attendant had told her before: Time-lag was a harmless condition where the traveler experiences short-term amnesia. She wouldn't get her lost time back, but the amnesia wouldn't affect her any more. It was as if, the medical attendant had put it, her memories had been lost in translation.

She hadn't worried too much about it before. It'd just been one day, and the medical attendant said it was so rare that she would probably never have it again.

Except she did. She did have it again, and this time she'd lost two weeks.

Maybe there was something wrong with her. Maybe she was broken. *Shit.* That meant her career was over. If she couldn't travel through the teleportation network, she couldn't do her job.

The last time it had happened, the medical attendant had explained that the reason why all travelers on the tele-portation service were recommended to make a deposit at the memory bank was explicitly because of the rare chance of time-lag. But Kimiko hadn't been to the memory bank recently...had she? She'd been preparing for a trip to...not London. To South Africa. She'd been on assignment, to photograph the death of the last naturally born male African lion. She'd specifically gone to the memory bank in downtown Tokyo so that she'd be ready for the trip, on June second, the last day she actually remembered.

But she hadn't gone to Johannesburg. Or...she had, maybe? Those two weeks were completely lost to her. Maybe she'd gone, and then gone to London after that, and been fine, and then gone to Tokyo and done all that without going to a memory bank...but that wasn't like her. After she'd lost that day, Kimiko had been adamant about going to a memory bank before teleporting. She must have memories at the bank, even though she didn't remember depositing them. She'd go there, get her past back, and remember London and whatever had taken her there.

With shaking hands, she opened the lid of her teleportation-safe luggage box. It opened with a hiss, revealing the scant contents: a suit of clothing, some toiletries, and her cloud reader. Computers never travelled through teleports well; cloud readers were simple device that could just read information stored in the network.

After freshening up and dressing, Kimiko reached for her cloud reader, swiping it on and quickly looking for any clues as to what she'd been doing the past two weeks. She checked her schedule. It was oddly blank. Whatever Kimiko had been doing in London, she had to have done it for an assignment—it's the only reason she ever travelled. But there was nothing there—nothing in her schedule, nothing in her notes, no written reports, no collection of vids to upload later. It was as if the last two weeks had not only been erased from her mind, but also from her life.

Kimiko was about to drop her cloud reader back into her luggage box when she noticed something scratched faintly into the paint at the bottom of the case. She dropped to her knees and ran her fingers over the newly roughened surface.

Don't trust TPS.

Kimiko's eyes widened. The only person with access to her luggage box would have been her. And, of course, Teleportation Services, which scanned the contents for materials that couldn't safely teleport. If she had hidden a note or something for herself, they would have found it—but they could have easily missed this faint message.

A voice came over the intercom—a female voice that spoke with bland monotony. "Kimiko Murasaki, your teleportation attendant indicated that you needed medical attention. Please report to the medical bay before leaving the station."

Kimiko slammed her luggage box shut and headed to the door. It whisked open, and Todd the attendant stood waiting for her.

"I'm to take you to the medical bay," he said immediately as Kimiko strode past him.

"I'm fine," she said.

"But Ms. Murasaki—"

"I was just disoriented. I splashed some water on my face, and I'm fine now."

"It's a free service, and highly recommended—"

"I don't need it."

Todd grabbed Kimiko's arm, forcing her to stop. She glared down at his hand on her, then up at him, and he snatched his hand back as if burned. "Ms. Murasaki, if you made a deposit at the memory bank, it's a very simple procedure to restore your memories." He tapped on his scanner. His face fell. "It looks like your last deposit was here, two weeks ago."

Kimiko gave Todd her most gracious smile. "I'm fine, really," she said. "I don't need the memory bank anyway." She turned to face the huge glass doors that opened up to the streets of Tokyo. "Thank you for your concern," she added, glancing back at Todd for the first time, "but I've just been overworked lately. I'm home now. Some rest is all I need."

Todd opened his mouth to protest more, but Kimiko walked through the doors and disappeared into the crowded city.

When she got to her apartment, it was weirdly half-empty. A chair was missing from the living room, the only indication that it had been there remained in the indented places in the carpet where it had rested. Blank spaces on the walls indicated a seemingly random assortment of pictures removed. In the kitchen cabinets, most of the plates were still there; most of the glasses were gone.

Unfortunately, Kimiko remembered exactly why. Her boyfriend had used her absence as a way to cowardly sneak out of their relationship for good.

He was gone.

Kimiko let her luggage box stay on the floor by the door as she walked around the weirdly decimated apartment. He'd even taken the damn curtains. Sunlight glared through the tall windows, harsh in its brightness. He couldn't have left those, no. He'd always been so methodical, keeping track of expenses, making sure that bills were paid exactly 50/50 between them, down to the very last yen. Kimiko had picked out those curtains, a beautiful, colorful sweep of fabric made from old saris, but he'd paid for them. He'd paid for them, so he took them back, even though he never liked the damn things.

"Asshole," Kimiko muttered as she went to the linen closet, pulled out a couple of sheets that he'd left her, and threw them over the curtain rod, masking the bright light.

Kimiko collapsed on the sofa and clicked on her main screen. The wall opposite the couch lit up. After a quick biometric scan, the screen brought up all of her preferred homescreens: The news network, her personal feed, her public feed, her private schedule, her messages. Nothing from Tadashi. Typical.

Kimiko swiped away the messages, scanning her calendar. She had the highest security on her private network—unlike her cloud network, which was monitored by the government. She saw the date, more than two weeks ago, where she logged into the memory bank last. She saw the scheduled trip to South Africa. And then, about a week ago, there was one quick note: TPSHQ. *What the hell did that mean?*

The screen lit up, alerting her that Tadashi Subaru was calling. She contemplated ignoring him—why should she bother talking to him if he was going to just leave her like a thief in the night?—but she couldn't resist.

"Hey," she grunted at the screen.

Tadashi had the grace to look ashamed. "Okay, look, I'm sorry," he started.

Kimiko melted—just a bit. She waved her hand dismissively. "This hasn't been working for awhile," she said.

Tadashi visibly relaxed. "I know. And it's best for both of us."

"You could have left me the damn curtains."

Tadashi opened his mouth to protest, and with just that, Kimiko could feel another argument rising between them. The thought of it exhausted her. "*Anyway,*" Kimiko said, "it doesn't matter. So this is it."

"This is it." Tadashi paused. "When you get the bills for this month, just let me know what I owe. I'll pay for my use while I was there."

Kimiko waved her hand again. She didn't want to

count out the yen that existed as the last remainder of a three-year relationship.

"Did you find what you were looking for?" Tadashi asked politely.

Kimiko's head whirled around. "What I was looking for?"

"When you commed in from Africa, you seemed... agitated? About something big? A news article you just 'couldn't pass up?'"

So that had been the source of their last fight and his move out—Tadashi hated it when Kimiko went chasing down leads, especially when it left her from home for longer than expected.

"Where did I say I was going?" Kimiko asked.

Tadashi frowned. "Did you not end up going to London?"

"No, no, I did," Kimiko say quickly. "Did I tell you anything else?"

"No. Did you uncover something big? Another award for 'reporting' in your future?" That same mocking tone. She was glad they'd broken up, even if she didn't remember it.

"Maybe," Kimiko said. "Let me know if you remember anything, though, okay?"

Tadashi frowned. "Are you okay? Are you... You're acting strange, Kimi."

"Don't call me that," Kimiko said immediately. "I've got to go."

"Okay, b—" Tadashi started, but Kimiko hung up on him.

So, she had gotten a tip for something while in Johannesburg, and that had led her straight to London. She stared at the strange series of letters she'd marked in her calendar: TPSHQ. TPS obviously meant "Teleportation Services," so HQ was...

Headquarters.

Kimiko tapped into her screen the location of the main offices of the international network of Teleportation Services.

The chief of global operations was stationed in London.

"*Yatta*," she said under her breath, although she felt no joy at the discovery.

Kimiko paced her apartment. She had been on to something, something big. Something about Teleportation Services. Had she really experienced time-lag when she teleported from London to Tokyo? Maybe they'd done something to her to make her forget what she'd learned there.

She had a sixth sense about good stories—it was what made her one of the best reporters out there. And she could tell that this story was going to be huge.

Kimiko had scratched the message about TPS into the bottom of her luggage case. Clearly before her memory had been messed with, she had known she couldn't trust traditional means of communication. Nothing on the cloud, probably, too public. Her private schedule had only shown one series of letters, but she wouldn't have left a big message for herself there. So what would she have done...if she knew she was in trouble, how would she let others know, how would she keep the info safe...?

Her mother's network account.

Her mother had never been technologically advanced and hated using her network account. But Kimiko had set it up for her anyway, and she knew all the passwords. Her mother lived at an elderly care facility now, and hadn't checked her network account for more than a year, but Kimiko had kept it active as a sort of backup system for some of her files. If someone was watching her and her accounts, Kimiko wouldn't leave herself clues there—she'd use her mother's account, which had just as much security as her own, but was far more private and not somewhere most people would think to look.

Kimiko whirled around, clearing her account from the home screen and logging onto her mother's account. There were her backup files that she remembered dumping there, but there was also a new folder, one that had only been created a few days ago.

Kimiko opened the folder, her heart thumping.

Instead of notes—instead of any logical explanation—she found images.

Collapsing on the carpet in front of the screen, Kimiko stared at image after image, swiping through them, her mouth open in shock and disgust. Each of the dozen or so images showed a person...or what remained of a person. The best ones still looked alive, but horribly, grossly malformed. The faces looked melted, as if by acid, some with key parts missing—an eye, a jaw, a crescent-moon chunk of the skull. None of the bodies had all limbs still intact; they had arms or legs missing, in many cases just lumpy sacks of flesh dangling from the torso. A few of the bodies had all four limbs, but the were grotesquely placed in the wrong places—an arm sticking out of the front of a chest, or two legs protruding from one hip, a hand attached to a knee, or all four limbs dangling from the waist, like a creepy experiment to create a human octopus.

Kimiko raised a shaking hand to cover her mouth, swallowing back the bile rising within her. The last few pictures were the worst. Just mounds of flesh and protruding bones, slime and blood covered, bits of hair or random facial features slipping down the slippery pile of skin—a few teeth in one; an eye dangling off the side in another.

Her hands shaking, Kimiko scanned back to the first image. She couldn't get emotional. She couldn't let herself focus on the grotesque images. She had to be analytical. She had to know why she had kept these pictures, why she had hidden them, and what they had to do with Teleportation Services. She selected the least gross picture, the least distracting one, and forced herself to look past the mangled flesh of what had clearly once been a human. A human that may not have been that different from her...this one had the long sweep of dark hair like she did, the same narrow eyes and angled cheekbones, the same ears that stuck out like her father's had. But she didn't have her neck twisted around like an owl's, she didn't have shoulders set at such weird angles, she didn't have a tumor-like mangled sack dotted with cellulose for a left leg.

She shook her head, clearing her thoughts, carefully

ignoring the similarities between herself and whatever this person had been before. Instead, she blew up the picture, enhancing it and examining the background carefully. This was some sort of scientific or medical facility—the entire area could only be described as "sterile." She squinted, looking for any identifying features on the image, something that would tell her where this had taken place or who was involved. The victims here didn't have face anymore, not really, but maybe she could find a name.

Nothing jumped out at her. No handy logos, no identifying nametags on lab coats carelessly tossed over chairs in the background.

"Chikushō," Kimiko cursed under her breath.

Okay, there was nothing in the image. Maybe she could examine the data behind the digital images, find the location of where they were taken. If Kimiko had snapped these pictures, she always attached a GPS code to the file. She cleared the images from the screen, turning instead to the metadata attached to each picture.

Finally. Her own code was linked to the images. She had taken these pictures. Now to find out where...she uploaded the information into her own program, a system she coded herself.

Teleportation Services, Tokyo Station

She had taken these pictures less than half a mile away, at the medical bay of the teleportation station she had just left.

Kimiko stood outside the Teleportation Station, and she considered her chances of discovery. She had uncovered something before, something important, but she had lost all memory of that, either through a case of bad luck with time-lag, or a case of malicious intent, somehow, from the very place she was about to enter.

The glass doors slid open.

"Ms. Murasaki!"

This baka, Kimiko thought to herself, but she plastered a smile on her face as the attendant Todd approached her.

"I've decided that you're right," she said as pleasantly as she could. "I should see the medical bay."

Todd nodded as if he completely understood her plight. "Time-lag can be very confusing," he said, already punching something into his scanner. "If you'll follow me?"

He led her down a glass and tile hallway, and soon Kimiko could see the similarities between this medical bay and the one in the pictures she'd taken. She repressed a shudder. She didn't want to think about those pictures, even if they were what had brought her here.

"A medical specialist will see you here," Todd said, waiting by an open door. Kimiko stepped into the examination room warily, but it seemed...normal. No malformed, rotting bodies in the middle of the floor.

The door swished shut behind Todd, and Kimiko was left alone in the room. She immediately turned her attention to the room. Two doors—one she had entered through, another one in the opposite wall where, presumably, the medical attendant would enter. She sat down on the slick examination table that smelled faintly of antiseptic. Nothing seemed out of the ordinary here. The basics of first aid lined the top of one counter; a memory bank hook-up stood on the other side of the room.

The door Kimiko hadn't entered opened, and a slim woman of African decent entered. "Your records indicate that you're fluent in English," the medical attendant said in a questioning voice.

"Yes," Kimiko said.

"Excellent," the woman replied. Her nametag, just below the TPS logo, labeled her as Dr. Obi.

"Is something amusing?" Dr. Obi asked.

Kimiko shook her head. "Just that your name is common in Africa, but it also has meaning here, in Japan. An obi is a sash for a kimono."

"It means 'heart' in my homeland," Dr. Obi said with a smile.

Kimiko smiled. This was the sort of detail she loved about the world, the random ties that made it one. This is why she loved to travel so much, particularly with the teleportation stations that made the world seem small and accessible.

"So it seems that you experienced some time-lag after your trip today," Dr. Obi said, consulting her scanner. "But you left the facilities?"

"I was a little disorientated," Kimiko said, slipping immediately into the role of victim. "I didn't really understand what was going on."

"Your records show a previous instance of time-lag?"

"For only one day," Kimiko said. "I seem to be missing more time than that now."

Dr. Obi frowned, scrolling down Kimiko's information. "And you didn't make a deposit at the memory bank before your last trip," she said. "The last one was two weeks ago."

"That's the last I remember."

Dr. Obi looked at Kimiko sympathetically. "I'm sorry—without you having made a deposit at the memory bank, there's nothing we can do. Time-lag is rare, but when it occurs, it's simple to just upload your last memories if you've made the deposit."

"Lesson learned," Kimiko said, opening her palms in a show of defeat.

"But you were experiencing some disorientation as well?" Dr. Obi asked. She leaned closer, examining Kimiko's eyes.

"Nothing serious," Kimiko said. "How common is time-lag?"

"Rare," Dr. Obi said. "Only a fraction of cases are unable to recover lost memories, but unfortunately, those cases are almost all due to a lack of deposit at the memory banks."

"How many people have time-lag but are able to recover memories?" Kimiko pressed. "How often does someone need the memory banks?"

Dr. Obi shrugged, leaning back. "It's difficult to tell. If someone travels a lot, as you do, it's more common. It's a statistical anomaly, though."

"What causes it?"

Dr. Obi paused. "Why are you so interested in time-lag?"

Kimiko tried to look innocent. "I'm a reporter. We're a curious lot."

"I have some official press releases with the latest data I could send to you," Dr. Obi said. "I've only worked on a handful of time-lag cases, even though we have an in-house research facility here."

"Yes, please," Kimiko said.

Dr. Obi started tapping on her scanner. "What's your network connection?" she asked.

"Could I have a hard copy, please?" Kimiko smiled sweetly. By law, every business had to have paper records of vital information available to anyone who asked for it, but it was rarely requested. Kimiko knew it would take Dr. Obi some time to actually track down the paper to give to her.

"How are you feeling now?" Dr. Obi said.

"Fine, except for the amnesia, which you can't fix, right?"

"Sadly, correct." Dr. Obi headed to the door. "Stay here; I'll get you that information you requested." The door swished open, and Dr. Obi disappeared.

Kimiko counted to fifty, then jumped up and headed to the door. It was programmed to only open for personnel of the teleportation station, but Kimiko pressed her network connector to the lock, bringing up her unlock program. Reporters had to have the same skills as thieves; they were just after something more precious than gold or money.

The door slid open, and Kimiko crept forward. The

medical bay expanded into a series of offices and labs, but nothing immediately jumped out as significant. Kimiko swiped a spare lab coat by the door and shrugged into it, then brought up a blueprint of the station on her network connector. She scanned the room labels, and "time-lag research" was just two hallways away.

Kimiko walked as if she had every right to be in the private areas of the medical bay, striding confidently toward the labs. A few people passed—fortunately none of them were Dr. Obi—and soon enough, Kimiko stood outside the door of the research lab for time-lag.

Oddly, there were no lab technicians or scientists around. This area was completely empty. What had happened to the people Kimiko had seen in her images?

She pressed her network connector to the door, but nothing happened. The security here was higher than her little hack could handle. In that case...Kimiko worked quickly, enabling another hack that would disable the alarms of the building. It wouldn't work for more than half an hour, but if she couldn't do anything in that amount of time, she'd have to go anyway. Once she was sure the alarms wouldn't go off, Kimiko smashed her elbow into the biometric lock by the door and touched the manual door release.

She stepped inside the time-lag research lab.

The smell of antiseptic was even stronger here in the lab, as if it had recently been doused top-to-bottom with bleach. Kimiko immediately recognized the room from her pictures—the melting, disfigured bodies had been here. But now there was nothing but plain tile and chrome.

Counters and cabinets lined all the walls, and there were two other doors leading out of the room. Kimiko went to the other doors first—each one had a similar, advanced lock that her hack couldn't break. She pressed her face against the glass panes set into the door. One room was dimly lit, and all Kimiko could make out was a series of what looked like memory bank hook-ups. The other room was completely dark, but the label over the lock indicated that it contained the "Clone Replicator."

Kimiko frowned. What did clones have to do with teleportation?

She flipped through the cabinets in the main lab, but couldn't make heads or tails of any of the materials. But on top of one of the counters lay a stack of folders.

And the very first folder was labeled *Murasaki, Kimiko.*

Kimiko's heart dropped as she flipped the folder open. Her teleportation passport photo was attached to one side of the folder, as well as a chart of all her travels. Two of her travel dates were highlighted in the folders. The first was her trip about a year ago, the one where she had time-lag for the first time and lost a day. The other was her trip from London yesterday, with a note that she had lost two weeks this time.

She flipped through the file, trying to make sense of the medical language. And then an image dropped out, sliding over the smooth countertop.

"No," Kimiko whispered. "Masaka!"

It was the same image that she had hidden in her mother's network account, the image of the melted woman who had her ears and her hair and something like her face. Kimiko hadn't taken a picture of the woman—she had snapped an image from the file. From *her* file. She quickly moved to the other files on the counter—here were the dozen other pictures. She must have scanned them upon discovery.

Kimiko turned back to her own file, finding the place where the image was supposed to go, next to a report on her latest time-lag experience.

After journeying from London, Kimiko Murasaki experienced an extreme teleportation malfunction, resulting in irreparable deformity and the need for a clone replacement to be immediately replicated. Patient had no recent memory-bank deposit and was informed of 'time-lag.'

An alarm blared throughout the room—throughout the entire medical bay.

"Shit, shit, shit," Kimiko murmured. She swept the files back to a close proximity of how she found them, but the only way out of this lab was the door she came in—the one that led to the main hallway. Kimiko opened up the cabinet below the file folders, shoved the vials resting there to one side, and climbed inside, pulling the door mostly closed behind her.

Soon, a clatter of hurried feet on tile poured into the time-lag lab. "Why is this door already open?" someone asked, but apparently they weren't after Kimiko—they had an emergency, one that made them ignore the open door and the slightly ajar cabinet. Kimiko pressed her eye to the crack, trying to see what was happening.

The smell hit her first—a smell like burnt hair and rotting flesh.

"This one's still alive," a voice said.

"Document it, then put it out of its misery," another one said.

A flash of light—a photograph of the misshapen lump of flesh poured onto the tile floor.

"Is there something wrong with the teleportation portal?" a female voice asked. Dr. Obi. "This is the fourth case we've had this month."

"Nothing wrong," the first voice, an older man, said. "Just more people are using the teleporters more often. Statistically, we'll have more victims like this."

"It seems wrong," Dr. Obi said. "And I have a patient waiting for me—one who is asking questions about time-lag."

"Your patient can wait," the Old Scientist said. "This won't take long."

"I'll go to the clone replicator," a younger male voice said. Kimiko could hear him walking across the lab, and the door she couldn't see into opened.

The disfigured person moaned on the floor. Kimiko forced herself to look at it, at the place where an arm should be, at the caved-in chest, at the spotty patches of hair clinging to the lumpy skull. She forced herself to look, and to remind herself that this was a person.

"Wha...happen?" the thing that had been human asked.

"Mr. Jefferson," Dr. Obi said, kneeling down in front of the being with compassion in her voice. "There was a...

problem with your teleportation from Los Angeles. You're in Tokyo now, but you're...injured."

The thing—Mr. Jefferson—wheezed, a panicked, wet sort of sound.

"The damage is not irreparable, and we're working to bring you back to good as new," Dr. Obi said. "Trust us."

"Ready?" the Old Scientist said.

Dr. Obi stepped back. A moment later, an electrical blast vibrated across Mr. Jefferson's uneven flesh. He wheezed again—the closest thing he could come to a scream of pain—and then he was silent.

He was dead.

"The clone replication is ready," the Young Scientist said, emerging from the other room. He pushed something on wheels into the main lab, and Kimiko got a glimpse of smooth flesh and clear skin.

This was the man Mr. Jefferson was supposed to be. Maybe thirty or forty years old, somewhat handsome, with his arms and legs where they were supposed to be, his face still recognizable as a human face.

"I'll load up the memory bank database," the Old Scientist said, heading to the other room.

The younger man and Dr. Obi stood in front of the cloned replication of Mr. Jefferson's body. "So, we just load the memories that Mr. Jackson—"

"Jefferson," Dr. Obi corrected.

"Load his memories back up into this cloned body, and then boom, just like that, he's basically reset as someone who he was just before going to the teleportation station. And he'll never know what happened?"

"Just like that," Dr. Obi confirmed. "Teleportation isn't perfect. When it messes up, well…" she indicated the mess of what used to be Mr. Jefferson.

"And he won't know?"

"He won't know. As long as his memory banks were up-to-date, it'll be like nothing happened."

Kimiko bit the back of her hand, trying to suppress the urge she had to run screaming from the room. *This* is what had happened to her. She had had a bad trip in the teleporter, and had ended up as a monster of human parts. They had killed her and replaced her with a clone, reusing the last deposit she'd made at the memory bank.

"But what if the person hadn't been to the memory bank?" the Young Scientist asked.

Dr. Obi shrugged and moved away from the two Mr. Jeffersons. "Not our fault. We tell people to get back-ups done. And, of course, sometimes it works to our advantage."

"Our advantage?"

"That patient I had, just before Jefferson's bad teleport. She's a reporter; she'd been at the global headquarters for TPS. All they had to do on the other side was push her through the teleporter without letting her back up her memories. She forgot learning about what time-lag really is, and we gave her a…a reboot. We deleted everything before she started snooping into TPS. Now she doesn't know what she learned, and just thinks she had a routine bout of time-lag."

The young scientist whistled appreciatively.

Hidden in the cabinet, Kimiko swallowed back the

acid rising in her throat. *They had killed her.* They had made sure her memory wasn't backed-up, and they'd replaced her with an exact clone—but one more ignorant about what she'd been looking for. If she hadn't been paranoid, if she hadn't hidden clues for herself, she never would have known what she'd been doing in London, what memories she had lost.

And...holy shit. She considered the repercussions of this. Kimiko was just a reporter—but what if the TPS wanted to control someone important, like the leader of a country? People in politics travelled more often than Kimiko did, typically visiting a different region or country every day. If the TPS wanted to, they could easily erase the memories or replace any leader they wanted with a clone tweaked with leanings in favor of teleportation stations or whatever else they wanted.

Running footsteps skidded to a halt near the lab. "Obi, that patient you had—what happened to her?" the Old Scientist asked, panting.

"I left her in the examination room," Dr. Obi said. Her voice rose. "Why?"

"She's missing. And look—the door was forced open. The security alarms were disabled."

"Damn! She's a reporter—she's probably snooping around."

"And we've not gotten rid of Mr. Jefferson," the Young Scientist said.

"Do that, now," the Old Scientist said. "I'll upload the memories into the new Jefferson. Obi, you find your patient. You find her and make sure she hasn't discovered—"

"On it," Dr. Obi said with authority.

The three scientists moved quickly—the younger one dragging the deformed, dead body of Mr. Jefferson away as the older one pushed the gurney with the newly replicated clone of Mr. Jefferson toward the memory bank database. Dr. Obi moved to a screen on the wall, near the counters.

"Scan for unauthorized persons in the medical bay," Dr. Obi instructed the computer.

Son of a— the badges the scientists wear must have a chip in them; a scan would reveal someone without a badge hiding in the cabinet just a few meters away from where Dr. Obi was standing.

"Well, well, well..." Dr. Obi muttered, and Kimiko knew she was caught.

She didn't hesitate. Hesitation would ruin her. She threw open the door, leapt from the cabinet, and raced across the lab.

"Wait!" Dr. Obi shouted as Kimiko ran for her life. She skidded around the corner, down the next hall, and back toward the examination room. Dr. Obi chased after her, but Kimiko could hear her giving instructions into a communicator. If she could just get out, Kimiko could upload what she'd discovered, she could instantly put it on the network. The whole world would know in seconds. The teleportation services couldn't stop her. They couldn't stop the signal.

But she had to get out first.

Kimiko ran through the examination room—straight into Todd.

"Out of the way!" she screamed, shoving him aside as she darted toward the main entrance of the teleportation station. Red lights and an alarm were blaring now, strobing over her racing body.

The doors were sealed shut. A group of attendants blocked the main exit.

Kimiko skidded to a halt. *Shit.*

"Grab her!" Dr. Obi was just behind Todd, pointing. Todd ran harder toward Kimiko.

Kimiko spun around, heading deeper into the teleportation station. People—travelers who'd just arrived in Tokyo or were just about to exit—paused and stared gapemouthed as Kimiko sprinted past. She ducked into a portal room, breathing heavily, and turned to the empty teleporter platform.

She'd traveled hundreds of times. She knew the basic method. Quickly, Kimiko pulled her dress over her head and threw on a teleportation suit. She took a deep breath.

No other way out.

She spun the teleporter dial. Anywhere—anywhere but here. If she could just escape...she could upload info anywhere.

She just had to escape.

"Ms. Murasaki, please, stop," Todd said from the doorway.

Kimiko stepped onto the teleporter platform without even looking at where the dial would send her.

"Kimiko, there's really no point in running," Dr. Obi

said, following Todd inside. "Come down. We'll explain everything."

"And then you'll replace whatever I learn with my memory bank back-up from two weeks ago, before I started to see just what you did here," Kimiko snarled.

"Teleportation is dangerous," Dr. Obi said. "You've seen the results of that today. If you send yourself off, I cannot guarantee your safety. Malfunctions are...common in cases like yours. The teleporter may not work. They'll just replace you on the other side, and you'll be no better off."

"And I should tell you," Todd said, "you led us straight to where you hid your data previously, on your mother's network. We've already wiped it."

"So please," Dr. Obi said. "Don't make this harder for us. Just step down. You teleport now, and nothing changes. It'll malfunction, we'll reset you. It's just a matter now of whether we reset you in—" Dr. Obi checked the screen Kimiko had randomly set the portal to. "—In Siberia, or we reset you here."

Kimiko weighed her options. She may...she may have a chance to run, if she made it to Russia. Maybe.

But if anything went wrong, everything was lost. She hadn't been to a memory bank, and it didn't matter anyway —the TPS controlled them. Just like they controlled whether or not they'd bother reuploading her into a new clone replicant. Maybe it'd be easier to just let her die a monster. A scandal now of a single victim who didn't survive a teleportation would be easier for them to deal with than her revealing to the world the chance of having your body replaced by a clone just for a quick vacation to the next country over.

But...they may not actually cause the teleporter to malfunction and leave her as a lumpy, Frankensteinian monster. If they didn't do that, if they didn't get in touch with the Siberian Teleportation Station in time...she could run. Maybe.

Kimiko slammed her hand on the teleportation initiation.

Test Facility Site:
  Nabco Research Station B

Test Administrator:
  Dr. Richard K. Philip

Test Subject Identity Code: ES42

Test Administered: Turing

"DO you know why you're here?" Dr. Philip asks.

I laugh. "I would be rather stupid if I didn't."

Dr. Philip's smile is indulgent, which frustrates me. I

uncross my legs at the ankle and re-cross them at my knees, not bothering to readjust my skirt. Dr. Philip blushes and looks down at his clipboard.

"I need you to state your reasoning," he says. "For the record."

He might be a professor, but he isn't much older than me. Not more than a decade. Just about right.

"My name is Elektra Shepherd," I say. "I'm eighteen years old. A freshman in university majoring in artificial intelligence. Today I am a participant in a Turing test. For the record," I add in a lower voice, just so I can see Dr. Philip blush.

"Thank you, Ms. Shepherd," Dr. Philip says.

I smile at him, relishing the feel of my heavy lipstick on my lips.

"And could you state what you think a Turing test is?" he adds.

I raise my eyebrow at him.

"For the record."

"A Turing test is a test developed to determine whether or not artificial intelligence has, well, *intelligence*. Essentially, a person—me, in this case—is separated in one room. Across that wall," I point to the wall directly oppo-site me, "is another room. Inside the room is one person and one AI. All three of us are going to have a little conver-sation, and then I'm going to tell you which one the person is."

"Which one you *think* is the person," Dr. Philip says, making a note on the paper in his clipboard.

I roll my eyes. "Come on, Richard."

"Dr. Philip, please."

"Come on, *Dr. Philip.* I know I'm just a freshman, but I think I'll be able to figure out the difference between a computer and a person."

Dr. Philip laughs, and something in the harsh sound makes me uncross my legs and readjust my skirt. "Oh, you'd be surprised," he says. "AI has come quite a long way in the last five or so years."

I have a dozen witty comebacks for his words, but not one for the sneering tone of his voice.

"Shall we get started?" Dr. Philip asks.

"Let's," I say.

Dr. Philip does a sound check on the microphone and a visual check on the video recorder that will be monitoring me. The two screens on the wall across from me light up. SUBJECT BLUE, the first screen says in bright blue letters across the top of the black screen. SUBJECT RED, the other screen says.

TESTING...TESTING...TESTING... flashes across both screens at the same time.

"I'll be just on the other side of the door if you need anything," Dr. Philip says as he opens the door. I nod. He shuts the door, and I hear a lock click into place.

The two screens across from me fade to black.

A minute goes by.

"Hello?" I finally say.

"Hi!" flashes in bright blue letters across the screen on the left.

"Hey," flashes in duller red letters across the screen on the right.

"Let's begin," I say.

"Let's," says Blue.

"Okay," says Red.

I glance at the video recorder in the corner of the room, aware that Dr. Philip's eyes are on me right now. It makes me uncomfortable, as if I were the one being tested, not Red and Blue.

"Well, I guess the obvious question is...are both of you human?"

"Yes," says Blue.

"Obviously," says Red. "But then again, if the whole point of this test is to trick you, then I'd of course say that I was human, even if I wasn't."

I lean forward, smiling. "Well, I wouldn't want you to make this easy on me."

"That's not a question," Blue says.

"I would like to make this as difficult as possible for you," Red says.

"Okay..." I think fast. "What's the square root of four-thousand-thirty nine?"

Math has always been my strong point—if Blue or Red figures out this problem quicker than me, then that one must be AI.

"63.5531274," Blue says as I'm still figuring out the last numbers.

Gotcha, I think.

"I'm a math major, haha," Blue adds after that.

Maybe not.

"The answer is 62," Red says.

"Ha!" I laugh triumphantly, "The answer isn't 62! An

AI just has a fancy calculator for a brain, it would know the right answer."

"But," Red types quickly, his words forming on the screen as fast as I can read them, "If I were trying to trick you into thinking I was a human, then obviously I would tell you the wrong answer."

I narrow my eyes. "Then what is the right answer?"

"I don't know," Red says.

But, of course, that's what he would say if he was trying to trick me.

Math wouldn't work—basic knowledge wouldn't work. Even if Blue answered everything correctly from the year Columbus discovered America to the exact number of electrons in carbon, he could just be really smart. And even if Red failed every question I asked—he could just be getting them wrong on purpose to throw me off his scent.

Time to get personal.

"I'd to get to know you both better, " I say. "What're your names?"

"That's irrelevant," Blue says. "We're supposed to be anonymous."

"They call me Andy," Red says.

"We're supposed to be anonymous, huh, Blue?" I ask, smirking. "So I guess you're not going to tell me much more than that you're a math major?"

"I don't think I was supposed to say that..." Blue says.

"The computer told you he was a math major?" Andy says. "Funny. Bet he guessed the square root question so quick he had to throw you off with that."

I laugh—then I realize that by laughing, I'm already

thinking that Andy is real, not Blue, and I want to keep an open mind. Dr. Philip said the test would be tricky, and it is.

"What about you?" Andy asks.

"Me?"

"What's your name, major, all that stuff."

"I'm Elektra, a freshman in AI."

"AI!" Andy says, and even though the words are written across the screen, I can imagine his tone of voice: impressed with a hint of laughter for the joke of an AI major conducting a Turing test.

"Yeah," I say. "You?"

"Sophomore in engineering."

"What kind?"

It takes Andy a moment to respond. "What kind of sophomore? Just the regular kind, I guess."

I really do laugh aloud now. "No, I meant—what kind of engineering?"

"Oh! Haha. Android engineering."

"So you make robots?" I ask. There's a huge competition between my college and his—the running joke is that the AI college makes the brains and the android engineering college makes the body.

"Are we still doing the test?" Blue asks, and I'm reminded of why I'm here, and that Andy might not even be real.

"Enough background," I say, straightening up in my chair and assuming a more authoritative voice. "Let's discuss philosophy. What's the meaning of life?"

"What do you think is it?" Blue asks.

"That's a stupid question," Andy says. "It means something different for every person."

"Well, what do *you* think?"

"I think," Andy says. His words appear on the screen slowly, as if he's contemplating each word carefully. "I think that life doesn't have a meaning. It just is."

"That's kind of dark. So, is there a God?"

"Does it matter if there's a God?" Blue asks.

"An interesting question, considering what we're doing," Andy says.

"What do you mean?"

"Just...if there is a God...does that fly in the face of this test? Your major?"

"What, AI?"

"Yeah, artificial intelligence. I think you could make a case that AI invalidates the possibility of God."

"Why?"

"If man can make life—because, honestly, isn't AI life? —if man can do that, then what's the point of God?"

"This is not a religious debate," Blue says.

"You're right," I say, but Andy's words have thrown me off. I wouldn't say I was a religious person, per se, which is why I never thought of the way religion doesn't seem to co-exist too well with AI studies. But...AI is AI—it's not a human. "If artificial intelligence does gain sentience..." I say slowly, thinking about each word, "If, for example, Andy, you're the AI, but you trick me into thinking that you're human—if AI is so clever and intelligent that it could pass for human...does that necessarily mean it has a soul?"

"Why would a soul matter?" Blue asks.

"Because if it has a soul, then that means man has usurped God. But if it doesn't have a soul, then that means..."

"I don't know," Andy says. "But that's the line between AI and human, isn't it? A soul. Not intelligence. Soul."

And he has a point. It's not intelligence that will enable me to pick between Blue and Andy as to which is human and which is essentially just a trumped up computer.

"And have you seen what's been done in android research," Andy continues. "I've seen bits of it. Computer engineering, you know. And they can make an android now that has the exact same motor functions as a human. It's so precise. Pair the mechanics of that with the AI that people in your department are working on...you've got something that *looks* like a human and *thinks* like a human...so what's the difference between you and it?"

And suddenly I remember: the urgency Dr. Philips had in setting up this Turing test; the secretive nature he's had about it; the way everything, *everything* had to be "for the record." Maybe this is the breakthrough. If I were to open the door and go to the other room, would I see two things that look like a human? Two things that look so similar to me that I wouldn't be able to tell them apart, even though one has electronics and circuitry inside and one has bones and blood?

But I laugh, and in my laugh is the sound of relief. "But we're not that advanced yet," I say. "We haven't come close to pairing a realistic robotic android with an AI of adequate intelligence. In fact," I say, "have you noticed that every answer to my philosophical questions have been answered by a question from Blue."

"Excuse me?" Blue says.

"Another question. Big surprise. You've had to repeat everything I've said, or turn it around, turn it into a question for me. You can't add depth to the conversation, you can only string me along with equal questions. You can't do anything else because you can't think for yourself. Nice try, but I've done my research on Socratic AI's. Blue is the artificial intelligence, Andy is the human."

The lights in the room flash, and the screen with bright blue letters goes dark. Andy's red letters stay on.

"I've figured it out," I say to the room. "I'm done."

"No you're not," Andy says.

"What do you mean?"

"There's more to test."

"I don't understand."

"A simple Turing test is to figure out which one of two options is the human and which one is the AI. But that's too simple—and you're an AI major, after all, so you'd know about standard Turing tests. To make it more complicated, Dr. Philip has added another layer—there's a chance that both the other guy *and* me is AI, or that neither of us are."

I roll my eyes and sigh, but a thrill runs up my spine. A challenge.

"If you're AI," I tell Andy, "then you're very, very good."

Andy doesn't respond at first. "I wonder if the test is more than that," he says finally.

"What do you mean?"

Andy is silent for a longer time this time, so long that I start to get nervous that Dr. Philip has cut off his screen, too, and ended the testing, but the red cursor on his screen still blinks.

"How much do you know about Dr. Philip?" Andy finally says.

"He's Dr. Philip. What's to know?"

"How long has he been at the university? Who's he working for? When did he start studying AI?" Andy types this so quickly that I have a hard time reading the words fast enough; the red blurs together.

"Why are you asking these questions?"

"Test subjects should maintain focus," Dr. Philip's voice echoes across the room from the speakerphone.

My mind's racing, though. I met Dr. Philip only a few weeks ago, when he began looking for subjects to screen for the Turing test. When I think of him, I think of sterile labs and clipboards and questions.

Do I know him outside of the Turing test projects?

No.

Do I know where he came from?

No.

The university set the entire research project up. The university that has the most advanced android and AI programs in the nation...in the world. And two of the subjects in the test are an AI major and an android engineering major. What if I'm not testing

Andy...what if the university is testing both of us? To see if...

If Dr. Philip is such a good android that even we won't notice.

I eye the camera in the corner of the room. He's watching me...or maybe the university is watching me, waiting to see if I can figure this out.

"I'd like the test to be over now," I say.

"I'm sorry," Andy types on the screen, but before I can see what he's sorry about, it fades to black.

I hear a click, and the door opens. Dr. Philip enters, clipboard in hand. "Your final evaluation?" he asks. When I don't speak, he adds, "Do you think Subject Red is a product of artificial intelligence?"

"No," I say, looking straight into Dr. Philip's eyes.

"For the record, your final standing is that Subject Blue was AI, and Subject Red was not?"

"Yes. For the record."

A small smile twists the corner of Dr. Philip's mouth. "Very good. Now, if you wouldn't mind turning that way." He points past me.

"Why?" I ask, immediately suspicious. If I turn the way he's indicated, I'll have my back to him, and something about this entire project has me deeply afraid that if I turn my back to Dr. Philip, something horrible will happen.

But he smiles at me, and in that smile, I remember the easy way he would speak to me during the lab sessions before the official test, the way he told me once about his wife and young daughter, and I think to myself: no. Surely not. He's not an android with AI. He's human, like me.

I turn around.

Everything goes black.

Test Facility Site:
Nabco Research Station B

Test Administrator:
Dr. Richard K. Philip

Test Subject: Rory Rivers

Test Administered: Turing

"Do you know why you're here?" Dr. Philip asks.

"Yeah," Rory says.

"Could you state your role in the Turing test? Speak up, please; the microphone is here."

"My name is Rory Rivers. I'm a junior at State."

"Your role in the Turing test held today?" Dr. Philip prompts.

"I was Subject Blue."

"And could you tell us a little bit about your experience?"

Rory shifts in his chair. "Do we have to do that with...*that* here?"

Dr. Philip makes a note in his clipboard. "Does it disturb you?"

"Shit yes. It looks effing *human*."

The doctor makes another notation. "Good. That is, of course, the goal."

Rory swallows, his Adam's apple bobbing up and down.

"I need your account please. For the record."

Rory nods and rips his gaze away from the thing slouched in the corner of the room. "I was Subject Blue, like I said." He bends closer to the microphone in the center of the table. "I was told to give really short answers to all the questions and to use a computer to help me with answers if I needed one. I was told—*you* told me—that I should be really focused in the questions."

Dr. Philip nods. "And you were quite good at that role. Thank you."

The door opens. A tall, thin man enters. He's wearing a lab coat just like Dr. Philip, and a broad grin slices across his face. "A success, don't you think?"

Dr. Philip nods and turns off the microphone. He checks his clipboard. "The subject displayed a wide range of reactions. Curiosity, reasoning, philosophy, logic. Even paranoia and fear."

The tall man's grin turns into a smirk. "And even romantic interest there at the beginning, I think."

"Who are you?" Rory demands. He's unnerved by everything that's happened today. He signed up for the Turing test because it was an extra $200 credited to his university account, but he hated the mind games being played.

"Sorry, didn't mean to be rude!" the tall man says

jovially. "I'm Dr. Andrew Deckard." His eyes light up. "Andy. Subject Red."

Rory stands and shakes Andy's hand.

"And I see you've met Elektra Shepherd," Andy adds, nodding toward the *thing* in the corner.

Rory glances back at it. It's beautiful—for a robot. Long, graceful-looking legs, slender arms, wavy dark hair. The eyes stare openly—a vivid, clear shade of hazel—but there's no light in them. If Dr. Philip were to go back to the android and flip the switch on the back of her neck, though, Rory had little doubt that the thing would come alive and speak as animatedly as it had during the Turing test.

"She's our pride and joy," Andy says. "Model #ES42. Our first sentient android. We've been working on her a long time, and she's pretty much perfect."

"What will happen when you turn her back on?" Rory asks. He stares at the android with a sort of horror-filled fascination.

"She'll pick up immediately. She's designed to assess the situation before sentience is fully booted up, then her artificial intelligence creates an artifice for her. She'll believe her situation is real and valid."

"What Dr. Deckard means," Dr. Philip says, stepping into the conversation when he sees Rory's confused face, "is that we've constructed her intelligence in much the same way dreams operate. When you dream, you believe the scene you're in is perfectly reasonable. Perhaps you dream that you're in a classroom—if you were aware of the dream and questioned, you'd realize you have no memory of how or why you got in the classroom. ES42's reasoning works the same way. If Andy had probed her for details on how she got in the room and got set up for the test, her artificial intelligence would supply her with some answers—give her just enough information to make her believe that it was perfectly logical for her to be where she is now. But if pressed, she couldn't tell you what the outside of this room looks like because, frankly, she's never been outside."

"We're displaying her at the International Research on Android and AI Studies Seminar at the end of the month," Andy says, pride ringing in his voice. "When we turn her on there, she'll process the situation quickly and create a reason in her AI for being there. She'll probably think she was an assistant to Dr. Philip on a project or something similar. And she'll just blend into the scene."

Dr Philip laughs. "I suspect that many of the other scientists won't even figure out she's a sentient android until we reveal at the end of the seminar!"

Rory, however, can't take his mind off her clear, ringing voice, the way she asked about souls. Andy had said that life meant something different to everyone, and it was only now, in seeing the hollow shell of Elektra Shepherd—of Model #ES42—that Rory realized just how true those words were.

SIX

MALFUNCTION

THERE WERE WORSE jobs in the universe.

It helped, of course, that Lyka didn't really mind being alone. And the money was good—very good, since she also didn't have to pay for room or board while on the portal station. But it was the *time* Lyka was really after. Ten month stints as a malfunction watcher during portal and terraforming development meant ten months of solitude, and that was *exactly* what she wanted.

Lyka's current deep space station was the jump point, the center of a hub of networked portals that stretched across the void of space. For the most part, she worked in the hub as an engineer, but whenever the opportunity arose, she'd hire on for the long, lonely jobs—three or five month stints at a portal station or a terraforming grid. This job—a ten-month gig as a malfunction watcher—was one of the last opportunities for such a long solitary assignment. The network was almost complete; the portals already operational, with no plans to extend out even further.

Turns out there was a limit to how far humans wanted to go into the dark, and this last portal station was it.

The station orbited a large moon that was, in turn, orbiting a gas giant in a binary star system that somehow, despite having two suns, was still cold enough to turn the moon into ice. But the salient point was that the ice was made of clean hydrogen-dioxide, a viable planet for terraforming and colonizing.

The portal was pretty much done thanks to the bots, each equipped with level-one artificial intelligence. It had been remotely inspected and tested, but Lyka still had to sign off as the first human to step foot onto the portal station, her bioscan and signature proof that she accepted the risks, understood the possibility of portal malfunction, and would not sue any of the manufactures who were sponsoring her position.

Lyka wasn't too proud to admit that she was hungover when she signed the screen and pressed her forehead against the scanner for an eye read. Usually an introvert, she'd bounced from club room to club room last night in order to get any trace remains of desire for human contact out of her system.

She hadn't been trying to forget anything, nor had she been trying to grapple with fear, which is what her friends had all assumed. She understood that she was basically signing up for solitary confinement (even level one AI didn't make up for human interaction). Lyka had no one and nothing to miss by signing up for the job—even her friends were little more than glorified age-appropriate work acquaintances. If anything, her last bender before departing was her way of confirming that the deep space station was not her home, that she could forget it as easily as she forgot the night with enough jet juice and star sparkle down her throat.

Lyka had slept through the first hops—the hangover was good enough for that. The final stretches as she went from portal to portal had been done in a migraine-blinding haze. But she forced herself to focus now as a worker at the last portal—himself coming off a ten month stint—checked her through.

"This isn't my first time," Lyka had reminded him. His name was Wolnit. He wore his loneliness like a hooded cloak that shadowed his eyes; his need for human interaction was evident in every twitchy movement.

"I have to go over it all," he said, although Lyka suspected he spoke merely for the pleasure of being listened to. She would not need that at the end of her ten months, she was sure of it. As he went over the final rounds of regulations and statistics, Wolnit's tone was an exuberant mismatch to the dull words he read from the screen.

Portals had been a way of life for generations, but trial and error had brought forth a plethora of red tape. Fair enough, Lyka reasoned; error in space typically meant at least one life was lost. But the practice of building portals to new colony worlds had become so regulated that the job of the malfunction watcher wasn't even necessary except for the laws that required one living, breathing, actual human to ensure that the bots had someone to override any issues. Level one artificial intelligence meant that the drones could analyze and self correct any minor issues, and the technology was advanced enough that no malfunction watcher had been needed in years. Still, *if* something happened, Lyka would be on hand to reset all functions. She was a glorified lifeguard in the sea of space where all the swimmers were programmed to be experts.

Or something like that. Hangover migraines were the worst.

"Of course, you have triple the supplies you need on hand at the station already in position," Wolnit said, reaffirming the same documents she'd already signed twice—once when she accepted the job, and again just before she'd left. He held a scanner pad out to her. "And there are three medical droids, should you incur injury."

"I *know*," Lyka said, already pressing her eye against the scanner.

Wolnit stared at her a beat too long. *It really has been awhile since he's seen another human,* Lyka thought.

"Do you know?" Wolnit asked softly.

"This isn't my first gig."

He glanced at her data pad. "You've done a handful of threes and fives. The long ones are different."

Lyka shrugged.

"It gets in your head," Wolnit said. She noticed that he positioned himself in front of the camera, and he spoke in low tones. The company didn't record everything—there was no point, really, since it would take too long for a video feed to travel the light years back to the deep space station. But pass-offs like this, where a person had one last chance to back out of the gig, those were recorded. Liability, probably.

"The first few months are fine," Wolnit continued. "Hell, the first half a year. It's around month eight or nine —when you're so close to escape. That's when time seems to crawl." He shivered, as if his analogy were literal, time taking spider-like steps over his skin.

"I'll be fine," Lyka said loudly. She put the scanner, already flashing green with her acceptance of the risks, on the table between them.

Wolnit shrugged, giving up on her. As soon as she was through this portal, he was going to be able to go the other way, taking the route from jump to jump all the way back to the deep space station. His time was up. His bank account was fat with savings, and he could take a vacation surrounded by as many people as he wanted now.

After formalities were taken care of, Wolnit showed Lyka to the last portal. "It shuts down after you," he said, something else she already knew. There was no going back. Not for ten months.

Lyka didn't look back.

———

Silence was an old friend to her, and, aware of the rigors of solitude, the company had provided her with lots of entertainment feeds and music files. She didn't bother with them, mostly.

She had a plan.

Monitoring the malfunction risk of the bots didn't

require much attention—her job was to react to a problem, nothing more. As long as things plugged away as they should, which they did because the machines were reliable, there was nothing to do.

Which was why Lyka intended to use this time for art.

Art wasn't unheard of, even in the work-focused deep space jobs, but one could not be *only* an artist, not on a station that didn't care how beautiful a thing was if the seal around the airlock wasn't tight enough. Lyka had done the practical thing and worked in engineering to pay the bills, but she used her digital pad to draw in her spare time, and she watched instructionals more than any entertainment feed. Work came first, though, diagrams before drawing.

Lyka was certain that, given the luxury of time and silence without the worry of how to make ends meet, she could produce the type of art she had always wanted to. She could not drag an easel into a hayfield as the Impressionists had done; she did not have patrons like the Renaissance artists; she could not break something functional and call it art like the Dadaists. In space, she was trapped behind walls and every spare meter was used to maintain the survival and work environment of the inhabitants.

Here, though?

The portal station was vast, intended to maintain a crew of several dozen and process all the colonizers that came through. Outside, in the void of space, bots worked on the various terraforming mechanics that must be completed. Screens along every wall in the station showed that all was going well, no need for her interference or override. Later, once the terraforming was done and this moon was ready to be colonized, an entire team of port authority workers would man this station, with the screens lit up with portal transferrals as the moon became not just a side job but a permanent home for people.

Lyka had a sleep pod, but there was no one to tell her not to claim the entire portal station as hers. She went where she wanted. She stretched her arms as far as she could, and she touched neither walls nor another crew member.

It was *glorious*.

The company had provided an advance so that participants in the work program could spend their time in activities best suited for them. It was how she'd finished her engineering degree a few years ago—downloading courses and reading the entire textbooks during the shorter gigs was the perfect combination of focus and time that let her skip ahead. Now, rather than lecture downloads and textbooks, Lyka had requested art supplies and instructional feeds.

She found them waiting for her in the storage unit by the portal hatch, a little card with her name on them. It wasn't much. Three canvases, a box of oil paints, rudimentary brushes, one sketch pad, half a dozen pencils. A bottle of varnish, a bottle of turpentine. Not much. But enough. More than she could have bought with her savings if she hadn't taken this job. Cotton didn't grow in space, not with synth fabrics being stronger and cotton being such a glutton for water. The canvas, pigments, oil, and brushes all had to be imported in from primary worlds. Even paper wasn't to be wasted with something as idle as a doodle.

There was a certain irony to it all, Lyka supposed—she was working on a station that was enabling one of the last funded exploration colonies, at least for her generation. And her job was allowing her to explore art and the possibilities of creation, one of the last chances for her to truly close herself up for nearly a year and discover all she could about herself and what she could do.

———

Lyka started screaming at the walls in the third month.

It wasn't because of loneliness.

She had yet to remove the plastic wrap around the pristine canvasses, nor pop open the tubes of oil paint. Her sketchbook was half-filled with pencil markings marred by eraser smears.

Nothing was right. She drew what she saw—her sleeping pod from the inside, the clean lines of the cabinets in the mess hall where her meals were stored. She'd drawn the curving expanse of the observation gallery, the one touch of beauty amidst the functionality of the portal station. Several pages of sketches tried to capture the view outside, the round moon and the planet beyond, the impossible stars stretching into forever.

It was all soulless. What was the point of art if all she did was render what was visual? Part of being an artist, Lyka knew, was her viewpoint. It wasn't enough to have the technical skill to render a photorealistic image with nothing but her hands. The choice of her subject mattered, the way she framed it, the focal point. She knew she had the hands for art, but did she have the eyes?

Lyka spent most of her time in the observation gallery, even spending some nights curled up on the tile. The curving carbonglass window stretched from floor to ceiling, a bubble just deep enough that, if she stood in the center, it was possible to blink away the rest of the station. Her stomach swooped in a way that almost made her nauseous as she walked right to the edge of the window. Her toes, covered in nonskid slippers made of polysynth material, pressed up against the seam where the carbonglass met the white tile floor of the gallery. Lyka leaned forward to touch the concave window in front of her, and when she looked down, she saw nothing but the void.

A little huff of air escaped her lips, and bile rose in her throat.

Yes. Here was her subject.

Not the portal station, not the black space it floated in.

No, she would paint the window. The emptiness outside, the reflection inside, and the glass itself.

The choice made, Lyka drug two tables into the gallery, one for supplies, one to work on. She should have thought to ask for an easel, but it was far too late to submit a request. She made do with an upside-down chair propped up on the table and meal packets as weights.

The canvas stood on this makeshift easel for two full days before Lyka picked up a brush, but even then she didn't load it with paint, despite the fact that she had everything in front of her to do just that. Blacks and blues, pale green and frosty white for the moon and stars, swirling russet and brown for the planet that was some-times visible. She had made a few sketches and knew she wanted to start with space, then the outlines of the ship. The reflection would come last, the mundane over the wondrous, a reminder of the limitations of the liminal.

Lyka flexed her fingers, the joints stiff, needing to pop but too swollen to do so. With her dry brush, she swept a stroke onto the canvas, imagining the line that could have stained the white had she the courage to dip into the paint.

Why was she hesitating so much?

Lyka could either poke at that thought or do the thing she had come to do. Action was better than self inspection; she grabbed the tube of black, popped the seal, and squeezed a line of oil paint directly onto the canvas, swirling her brush immediately into it, the tiny synthetic hairs carving little grooves into the darkness.

She held her breath as she pulled and pushed the color, forming the shape of the window. Sighing, she stepped back.

There was no going back now. The paint was spilled, the art begun.

Lyka gagged, turning her head away from the painting just before the contents of her stomach splattered onto the tile floor.

———

She focused so much that she started to develop headaches. Food became a necessity that she scarfed down only when her body would not function any longer without it—and even then, it churned in her stomach, acid boiling inside her.

Lyka had thought that selecting a topic to paint would help, and to a certain extent, it did. When she painted, she became lost in the canvas in a way she never had digitally. She spent two days adding fine detail to the grout lines of the tile; nearly a week on the rivets around the curving carbonglass window.

The headaches got worse.

Lyka delayed going to the med droid. Two were in storage; one was always ready at the charging dock. She'd had good health all her life, took her vits religiously, and had done her annual screen before she'd left for the gig. And… well, level one artificial intelligence was *weird*. To talk like a human, to react and ask questions like a human, but to lack any real feeling—it wasn't just edging on the uncanny, it fully threw itself into the valley.

She worked around the migraines. The aching body pains went away when she stretched and exercised.

Art helped her to disconnect from her own body. She was not a person painting, but a hand holding a brush, a finger directing it, a single nerve applying pressure. Lyka had spent her entire life being a whole person; she reveled in the sensation of being merely a sum of her parts creating something that existed beyond the corporality of her body.

In the fourth month, though, she realized she was late.

Lyka paused mid-stroke, her eyes unblinking. Portal hopping did a number on a body, but surely four months should have had given her one menstruation cycle at least.

She put her brush down without washing it. Red paint

leaked onto the table as she stood. Lyka stared blankly ahead—not at the painting, not at the window, but at her own reflection.

At the fear and doubt in her own face.

Lyka turned on her heel and walked straight to the medical bay. The lights automatically turned on when she stepped into the room, and the medical droid chirped out a little bell tone to indicate that it was coming online. Lyka sat down on top of the examination table.

"Hello, patient!" the medical droid said in a moment, its booting processors fully functional and receptive.

"I need a full scan," Lyka said. Her heartbeat thundered in her ears. How could she have thought herself a disconnected conglomeration of body parts? She was whole, she *here*, fully aware of how her entire self was united, blood and veins and bone and nerves, all of it wrapped around the core of her, the hard lump that existed not inside her stomach, but below it.

"Records indicate that you arrived one hundred and three solar days ago," the med droid said. "You should have checked in for a scan within your first seven days at the portal location."

"Okay, well, I'm checked in now," Lyka said. She held out her arm. "Do a blood scan."

"Have you experienced any negative health symptoms since your arrival at this portal station?"

The nausea. The headaches. The stiff joints.

"No," Lyka said.

The medical droid attached a sensor to her shoulder and another at the base of her neck. Lyka didn't feel the sting of samples being taken, and she barely registered the data that the medical droid told her about her insulin levels or cholesterol. "Positive serum beta-human chorionic gonadotropin," the medical droid said with no inflection. "Human pregnancy has been detected. Further testing is advised."

Lyka's whole body stilled.

"To help us determine which tests and supplemental vitamins or possible medication to recommend, please give me a brief history of your sexual conduct," the medical droid continued.

"I can tell you exactly when I got pregnant," Lyka said. She didn't need a calendar to check the date. She had drunk so much the night before she left for this portal station job that she didn't recall, exactly, if she had had sex nor with whom. There were a few possibilities, a few vague memories through the haze. Lyka choked back a sob. She had been with friends, or, at least, work friends, none of whom would have considered a fling any more than that. Nali treated sex casually; did he know that Lyka wouldn't have done anything had she not been drunk? Would he have cared? What about Huck or Sawrick? She could have DNA testing later to determine if any of them were the father.

Her mind spun. *Had* she been that drunk? She had felt safe, free—about to escape into the void. She hadn't thought about any consequences; she hadn't...

"Your heart rate is increasing," the medical droid said.

"No shit," Lyka muttered. But she took a deep breath. Another. She shut her eyes.

When she opened them, the medical droid was standing in front of her, waiting.

This wasn't going away.

Except...

"Abortive measures are still possible," the medical droid said, confirming Lyka's thoughts.

"I—"

"My sensors indicate that you are having difficulty processing this information," the medical droid stated. "Please do some calming activities and come back tomorrow for further discussion."

"Okay," Lyka said. She sat on the table. The medical droid stepped into the charging port, powering into standby mode. When Lyka didn't move, the lights dimmed.

———

There was more math to pregnancy than Lyka had anticipated.

She knew with certainty when a sperm had met her egg—there had been only that night, and none before, none after. Lyka decided it didn't matter whose sperm it had been, how it had come to be inside her. She *should* process that; she should poke into her memories, face what they said about the type of person who had seen her in that state, who had seen an opportunity. But she couldn't. Not yet.

Instead, she felt her body.

She hovered her hands over her stomach—a slight

bulge there, but not enough for her to have guessed, not really. Carbohydrate-dense meals and a lack of activity could have as easily accounted for the curve to her belly.

Her fingers pressed into her skin. Could she feel it? Could she hurt it? She snatched her hands away.

"There's no one here," Lyka said aloud. The medical droid had given her additional vitamins and supplements to take when she returned the next day. Day one hundred and four. Out of around two hundred and ninety. One trimester was over. She was already in the second trimester. There was no one here to talk to, to help her, to ease her mind or heart, to discuss her options—there was no one here.

Except her.

And the baby.

Numbers. She could focus on numbers.

Sex was day zero.

Discovery was day one hundred and three.

Pregnancy lasted nine months.

She didn't get to go back to civilization until ten months.

That meant... Lyka took a deep breath.

Less that six months. Less than two hundred days.

That was all the time she had before she was no longer alone on this station.

———

Lyka avoided the medical droid.

She shouldn't, she knew. There were tests to be done,

measurements to be monitored. Already her body didn't feel like her own.

It wasn't too late. That's what the droid had said. Not too late to make a decision.

To reclaim herself.

Lyka went to the observation gallery. The curving carbonglass window was the same; the bots outside building the terraforming grid over the moon the same. Her brush, saturated with red paint, was dried to the table, stuck like glue. The tubes of paint she'd been using were all sealed shut again—she was careful to conserve and protect her paint. But the red tube, the last one she'd been using, was still open. She squeezed the little bottle; the paint was hardened near the opening, but the end of the tube was still good. Maybe. She hoped.

Lyka sat down with a huff in front of her unfinished canvas. There were details still to be added, but the basic outline was there—the shape of the ship's window, the space beyond it. But the painting as it stood now appeared to show a gaping hole in the side of the ship, no glass, no barrier between the two places.

Her fingers hovered over the paint, the ridges made from thick oil, the thinned-out places where canvas still showed.

She'd come here to make art, not life.

She didn't *want* this. Not any of it, least of all the responsibility of making a choice. She just wanted to live her *own* life.

"That's my answer, isn't it?" she asked her painting.

It didn't feel selfish.

It felt like survival. A survival of the self she knew and loved.

But she didn't go to the med droid; she didn't ask for the drugs that would render the problem moot.

She sat and stared at her unfinished painting.

She wondered what she would paint in the reflection of the window that wasn't there.

———

Day one hundred and thirteen.

Lyka ignored every single ping from the medical droid requesting that she return to the med bay for further testing and monitoring.

But she also took the prenatal vitamins and supplements.

She looked at her body in the mirror; she weighed her breasts with her hands. She tried to see the difference within herself.

There was urgency in the way she painted, despite the fact that she was now working on the hardest, trickiest details. Lyka studied the Arnolfini portrait by Jan van Eyck, zooming in with her digital pad on the convex mirror where the artist had hidden a self portrait in the reflection. She got a metal bowl from the mess hall and inspected the way the shiny interior surface distorted her face.

She could still paint.

That had come as something of a surprise to her. Lyka could be both a painter and pregnant at the same time. It was such a simple conclusion, but—it's why she hadn't gone back to the medical droid. She could still *be*, some-how, despite also being more.

In her painting, the window's reflection showed the observation gallery in faint, ghost-like lines, but she had refrained from adding herself to the image, Van-Eyck-style, a hidden self portrait in the glass. Not yet. She wasn't sure why she hesitated—she had sketched her reflection often enough both in the digital pad and the sketchbook. She knew how to bend the shape of her body against the curve of the glass, but she still hesitated.

She stood up from the table she'd been working at, approaching the real window. She no longer saw the buzz of bots outside, the work of the new moon being prepared for a colony. She never looked down any more. Her eyes focused on the reflection. She could see everything clearer now that she was closer up.

The pregnancy itself didn't terrify Lyka. It was the month after. Ten months aboard the portal station meant one month by herself with a newborn. She had no clothes, no diapers—but she could make some from scraps of her own supplies. Food she could also make. She could...she could do this thing. It was unexpected and sudden, but... she could.

She could give birth by herself. The med bots were the best of the best, the newest innovations, designed to handle an entire colony of arrivals—they could handle one little baby arriving. There may be a bit of hubris to her attitude, but she also knew human births had happened for millen-nia. It could happen again. It could happen to her. She would boot up all three of the med droids, have them ready when the months grew long. And after birth—a whole month. It was daunting, but in a way comforting. For one month, the entire universe would be her and her baby. No one else. Just the two of them.

Lyka left the observation gallery, although she did pause to check that her oil tubes were sealed shut again. She could not afford to lose more paint.

Throughout her time on the ship—one hundred and forty-two days so far—she had not given much thought to her personal belongings. Lyka had little of her own mother. People didn't end up working on stations if they had an easy life with room to be precious about belongings. Her mother had taught her to be practical, had pushed her to ensure her own survival by any means, as she had done. But her mother had also bought her a fine point stylus for her digital pad and had spent money to print out Lyka's early drawings. After her mother died, Lyka had kept a scarf that had still retained some of her mother's scent. She had brought it with her to the portal station, and Lyka took it out now.

The long cloth no longer smelled of her mother, but it seemed right to make this be for the baby.

———

Although she had never liked med droids, Lyka supposed she should get used to them.

"Welcome back, patient!" the droid chirped as Lyka stepped inside the med bay. "You are due for several screens and testing."

"I figured." Lyka hopped up on the table.

"My preliminary exam merely detected blood hormones," the med droid continued. "But based on your own feedback about time of inception, these tests should be conducted. Please approve."

The droid held out its hand—human shaped, and covered in warmed synthskin—and a holo screen appeared above its palm, listing out a series of initial tests for Lyka's body to undergo, starting with a blood screen and an ultrasound. Lyka pressed her thumb into the droid's scanner, accepting treatment.

The droid applied med patches while it prepared an ultrasound. Lyka leaned back on the table, closing her eyes. Was she ready to see the face of her child? Was it too early? She had blithely skipped through her first trimester —would it have been better had she known?

A beep made her open her eyes and sit up.

"Please approve alternate treatment," the medical droid said. The holo screen had replaced the ultrasound test with a suggestion for a transvaginal ultrasound.

"What is this?" Lyka asked.

"Please approve alternate treatment," the medical droid said. "Preliminary bloodwork suggests the need for a clearer internal scan."

Lyka pressed her thumb in the scanner. "Is everything okay?"

"Your health is our primary concern," the medical droid said without inflection. "Please undress."

Lyka felt her heart rate pick up as she stood, and the beeping monitor nearby confirmed it. She quickly wriggled out of her clothing, tossing the articles into the corner. The droid had converted the exam table into a reclining bed with stirrups for her feet. Lyka laid down, not needing to be told what position to be in. Even though the medical droid narrated the procedure as it went, it felt invasive for the cold transducer to be inserted into her body. Lyka cringed, but even when she looked away, she could not escape the sensation of the rod, the pressure inside of her, painful as it prodded her organs.

When it was over, the medical droid offered a synth-skin-covered hand to help Lyka fully sit up.

"What did the scan show?" Lyka asked.

The droid's face shifted. It had been given a semblance of a human face, but it had limited expressions and no real transition from "neutral" to "sympathy" and back to "neutral." "We regret to inform you that the fetus is not viable," the droid stated.

"What?" Lyka asked.

The droid repeated the statement. "Testing has proven that a chromosomal duplicating error resulted in autosomal trisomy. No heartbeat is detected."

"What?" Lyka asked again, but she must not have spoken aloud because the droid did not repeat itself a second time.

"Recommended treatment: induced delivery and disposal," the droid said. "Do you approve recommended treatment?"

A little holographic screen hovered above the droid's hand.

"Already?" Lyka asked.

"Please approve recommended treatment," the droid said.

———

One hundred and forty two days. Lyka had calculated exactly how long a pregnancy would last, but had forgotten that, of course, sometimes it was less.

———

She looked inside the box the medical droid gave her, after.

She closed the box.

But the image would not leave her head. Not until she unwrapped another canvas. Not until she painted what she had seen.

She wrapped the box with the cloth her mother had worn. She put them both on top of her new painting, and set them on the floor of the hatch.

She walked out of the hatch and sealed the door.

Mechanics and engineering took over. The door was pressurized, and through the porthole window, Lyka watched as the light beside the outer door of the station flashed red, then green. The outer door opened, and explosive decompression sucked out the cloth, the painting, and the little box into space.

There one moment.

Gone the next.

———

Lyka returned to the deep space station at the end of her ten month gig. As expected, there had been no malfunction for her to oversee; the terraforming grid completed without a hitch.

The little moon was ready for human life.

At the last portal, Lyka recognized the operator—Wolnit, the malfunction watcher who'd completed his job as Lyka had begun hers. Rather than use his savings for a vacation, he'd accepted new work.

"How was it?" he asked. The franticness was gone from his voice now; he'd had a chance to use up all the words that had been bubbling inside him before. Through the porthole window built into the door, Lyka saw another man, a coworker waiting in the corridor.

Lyka didn't answer Wolnit immediately, and he laughed, a short bark that somehow evoked both sympathy and contempt. "I told you," he said. "Those ten month gigs are nothing like the short stints. They get in your head; they mess you up inside. How'd you keep busy?"

"I painted," Lyka said.

Wolnit blinked in surprise. "Art, huh?"

Lyka nodded.

"Well, let me see." The portal lit up, and a drone pushed through the crate that contained all of Lyka's belongings.

Wolnit's interest wasn't just in her painting, although she appreciated that he was being friendly about the mandatory inspection that anyone coming off a portal station job had to undergo. Some people, she'd been told, liked to take souvenirs from the job or got attached to company property during their stay.

Wolnit sifted through the crate quickly, then stepped back to allow Lyka to show him the canvases she had carefully packaged. His coworker, a tall man about twice her age, came inside, curious at the processing delay.

The company had provided her with three canvases. One, she sent into space. One remained blank—she did not yet have a painting to put on it. The other was complete.

"I don't get it," Wolnit said, staring over her shoulder.

"I ran out of red," Lyka said.

"Oh," the tall man said, pointing. "Look, it's a self portrait."

Lyka had painted herself in the reflection of the gallery window. Her image was distorted, not just by the concave glass, but also by the cloth draped over her face.

"You missed a spot," Wolnit said, pointing to the painted reflection's midsection, transparent and showing nothing but the black void of space.

Lyka didn't comment as the two men tilted their heads, staring at the painting. Eventually, Wolnit shrugged and handed the canvas back to her. She repackaged the crate, and the drone carried it, following her into the corridor as she orientated herself. She'd been assigned a room while her clearance papers for relocation were processed.

The two portal operators in the room behind her spoke in low tones but were not as quiet as they thought they were.

"Imagine," Wolnit told the other man, "you have ten

months in space to do anything you want, and all you do is paint a picture of yourself."

The tall man snorted. "How narcissistic."

Their laughter was cut off by the closing automatic door. Lyka glanced behind her at the porthole window, but she saw neither the men on the other side nor her own reflection.

SEVEN

AS THEY SLIP AWAY

1. Three Months before I Die

I STARE at the basket of hypodermic needles. So slender and pretty, each filled with a yellow liquid that reminds me of gold paint.

"Inoculations," I say. I consult the floppy that contains my instructions for today's labor. Across the top of the screen is a chart and the words GENETIC MODI-FICATION.

That's . . . not right. These needles are filled with inoculations.

Eldest told me so. That's what he said this morning, when he brought me the basket himself.

"Selene," he had told me, his voice warm and kind, "these are inoculations for the rabbits. Inject one full dose per rabbit today."

My eyes burn with pain as I scan the text on the floppy. There's nothing about inoculations here.

Sharp pain shoots through my head.

Eldest told me these were inoculations.

"Inoculations," I say, a soft smile curving my lips. I pat the basket of needles as if comforting it in the knowledge of what it truly is.

It doesn't matter what the chart and words on the floppy say. It only matters what *Eldest* says.

Everything is only what Eldest says it is.

———

The rabbit field is quiet, but not silent. That is what I like about it.

I like sounds.

Soft thumps on the ground as the rabbits hop around. The little chirruping noises they make. The gentle clacky-chewy sounds as they nibble on grass.

I sit down in the grass field.

For a moment, I look up at the sky. Made of metal and painted with clouds that never move. My sky is a certainty. That's nice.

Sometimes, I think about how I'm living aboard a spaceship hurtling through the stars toward a new planet. But those thoughts are too big, and so I don't think them often.

I blink and see darkness.

I open my eyes and see blue.

Blink. Dark.

Light. Blue.

Blink. Dark. Dark. I don't open my eyes. Dark.

Bloodbruisespainbetrayalalonealonealonealonealone.

I open my eyes.

I do not like the dark.

I stand. There is work to do.

The rabbits are fat and lazy. But they do not like it when I try to grab them. Perhaps they know that sometimes when I snatch them up, I send them to the butcher and they are made into food. But if they do know this, they're not *too* concerned about it. They scamper away, but only a meter or so. Then I sneak. I sneak behind them, where they can't see, don't know I'm coming.

They think I am their friend.

And then I lunge.

I tackle the nearest rabbit, pinning it down by its shoulders. After scanning its identification chip—*Number 424,* the screen says—I plunge a hypodermic needle into its back leg.

"Number 424, inoculated," I say aloud.

I don't have to say it aloud.

But I like sound.

This is my day. Sneak up on rabbits. Lunge. Grab. Hold. Inoculate.

Sometimes I look at the sky. Sometimes I look around me, at the green hills. I see someone running through the fields, a swing of color, bright against the normal green.

I hum, and I work.

And then.

Then a girl shows up.

She is a freak. Eldest told me she is a freak, told all of us on the ship. A genetically modified experiment gone wrong. She looks like a freak. Pale skin, almost the color of the fluffy white tails of the rabbits. Bright, bright hair. Red hair. With orange and gold in it.

Like the koi in the pond by the Hospital.

Friendsgonegonegonealonealonealone.

"Hello," the girl says.

I look at the girl. I look at her koi-fish hair. "Hello," I say.

She is different. She reminds me of . . . something. A sharp pain shoots through my head again. I look down, away from her.

"You're the genetically modified experiment," I say. I wait for her to confirm this is true, even though I know it is because Eldest said she is. "Eldest has said we don't have to speak to you."

The girl is mad at me. I know because of her voice. I like sounds. I pay attention not just to *which* words are said, but *how* they are said, and this girl says them angrily.

But she doesn't go away. She keeps talking to me. She asks about the rabbits. She asks about the needles.

She talks a lot.

"I saw you running," I say suddenly, realizing that the person I saw before was this girl, the bright color in the green fields was her koi-fish hair.

A strange feeling washes over me. My heart is loud and slow, and my head hurts.

"What were you running from?" I ask. My voice cracks. I pay attention to sound. Even the sounds I make. And the sound I am making is fear.

Hewillgetmerunrunrunrunrunhide.

"Just running," the girl says, as if it isn't strange to run for no reason.

She talks more. Questions, questions. I have work to do.

But then I remember more about what Eldest told us about this girl. That she was to live in the Hospital.

I ask her, and she confirms it. She lives in the Hospital.

"My grandfather was taken to the Hospital," I say.

Gonegonegone.

"Is he better now?" the girl asks.

"He's gone."

Gonegonegone.

"I'm sorry," the girl says. Her voice surprises me. She means it. She means that she's sorry.

"Why?" I ask. "It was his time."

The girl stares at me for so long I think she's done speaking. But then she says, "You're crying."

I touch my face.

My fingers come away wet with salty tears.

"I have no reason to be sad," I say.

It's true.

I have no reason to be sad.

None at all.

2. Seven Years before I Die

I suppose I should be upset that I'm crazy, but I'm actually quite pleased about it. Being crazy means I don't have to work in the fields or the City. It means I get to stay here, in the Hospital.

With my friends.

"Selene," Kayleigh drawls from the sofa in the common room. "Come sit with us."

Victria, who had been by the window staring at the open fields that separate the Hospital from the rest of the ship's population in the City, plops down in the center seat of the orange sofa made of scratchy wool. She wiggles in closer to Kayleigh, and the two girls look almost like sisters, with the same shade of olive skin and same length of dark brown hair. Everyone on the ship has similar coloring, but I think Victria tries to make herself into a shadow of Kayleigh. She deigns to glance in my direction. She doesn't *mind* me, exactly, she just likes to know the order of things. And the order of things here is that Kayleigh comes first, and Victria is always beside her, and sometimes, trailing at the end, is me.

It's almost time for lessons. Doc and the nurses like us all to take meds at the same time, just before the solar lamp in the metal ceiling clicks on.

"I hate the meds," Kayleigh says under her breath as Doc walks into the common room. He and the nurses distribute the pills, and we all swallow them down obediently. Except Kayleigh. She stares at the pill until Doc notices, and he doesn't look away from her until she gulps it down with some water.

I don't mind the Inhibitor pills, not like Kayleigh does. Swallowing one blue-and-white pill a day is a small price to pay for life at the Hospital. So we're loons. So we have to take mental meds. It's not so bad that Eldest keeps us here, removed from the rest of the ship, on the other side of

Godspeed, in the Hospital, away from the normal people. It's not so bad being abnormal here, where everyone else is weird too.

But if that pill is supposed to keep me from being crazy, it doesn't do a very good job. Instead of making me less loons, sometimes I worry it makes me more. I'm different. We—all of us in the Hospital—are different. I didn't have to see the way my parents' glassy eyes would flicker with concern when I spoke to know that the things I said weren't normal.

Doc says we're special, but "special" is just a nice way of saying "freak."

"Sometimes," Kayleigh whispers, "I think it's everyone else who's weird."

Victria's eyes dart around the common room, lingering on the nurses gathered around Doc by the door. One of the first things we learned was not to ask too many questions or draw attention to ourselves, and Kayleigh's words are incendiary.

"No," I say. "We're the freaks."

And we are. Everyone else on the spaceship *Godspeed* doesn't stay up late at night, worrying about whether or not the ship will ever land. They don't spend their time doing useless things like singing songs or drawing pictures. They never worry about whether Bartie will be able to rip his gaze off Victria long enough to notice anyone else. . . .

"We're not *that* freakish," Victria says. "I heard Elder takes the mental meds too."

I gasp in surprise. Elder, our future leader, is on mental meds like us? He's still young—living in the City now, awaiting the time until he comes of age and joins Eldest on the Keeper Level of the ship—but even the hint of madness in our leader disturbs me. "Will he come to live at the Hospital?"

Victria nods. "I heard Doc talking to Eldest about it. Elder will be moving here in a few months, after going to one of the farms for a bit."

I want to know more, but Kayleigh interrupts us.

"It's better. Being on the mental meds. I hated it before I started taking them," Kayleigh says. Her voice is clear and slow, as if she's measured the weight of each word and determined its worth before speaking it.

"You don't remember what it was like before. None of us do."

"I remember," she insists.

"Yeah?" My voice is a challenge. "What was it like?"

"Nothing."

"Tell us," I demand.

"Nothing. It was like nothing. It was like being empty inside."

Victria and I exchange a look.

"Sometimes . . ." Kayleigh sighs. "There's a lot about this ship that doesn't make sense."

"Liiiike," a voice calls out from the other side of the room, "how you won't let me kiss you!"

Kayleigh picks up a pillow from the sofa and throws it at Harley—not too hard, but hard enough. Harley tosses it aside easily, laughing. If I had to describe Harley as nothing but a sound, that would be it: *laughter*. He's always smiling, his white teeth unable to bite back the sound. He sees the world in shades of joy. Harley picks the pillow up from the ground, and I notice paint is caked under his nails, leaking out onto his fingertips.

"We were having," Kayleigh says, her voice punctuating each word, "a *private* conversation."

"Yeah, yeah, and meanwhile the rest of us are going to lessons."

"Going to lessons?" I ask, leaning forward. "But the lessons have always been here before." I don't know if there's much of a point in teaching crazy people things, but Doc insists that it's our duty to "hone our inherent talents." Every day, he or the nurses leads a discussion on topics relevant to studies: art, math, science. Things like that. And they're usually done here, in the common room, where there are enough seats for everyone and nothing to distract us from learning beyond the perfectly symmetrical and evenly spaced green fields outside the window.

"We're going to the Recorder Hall," Harley says, a mischievous light in his eyes.

Kayleigh rolls her eyes. "You made it sound like we were doing something important today," she says. "We've *been* to the Recorder Hall before."

"Yeah," Harley says. "But Doc's not doing the lesson there. The Recorder is."

My eyes grow round at this. The Recorder is going to teach us from now on? But . . .

"Why?" I ask.

Harley shrugs. A moment later, Doc starts calling out names. Harley was partially wrong: most of the other residents of the Hospital are going to lessons on the Shipper

Level. Doc tells them they're being apprenticed. It's people like Buck and Britne and Tailor—the ones good at the science and math lessons. People like me and Kayleigh and Harley—the ones who like art—are being sent to the Recorder Hall.

By the time Doc's done announcing our new roles and sending the studious ones to the Shipper Level, only a handful of us remain to go to the Recorder Hall.

"This should be fun," Bartie, Harley's best friend, tells me as we enter the elevator. I grin at him, hoping the heat I feel rising up in me isn't reflected in my cheeks. I can't rip my eyes from him until he turns to Harley and says something that makes him laugh, the sound of his voice jolting me out of my reverie. Victria shoots me a look, and my eyes drop to the metal floor of the elevator. I don't want her to know how I feel about Bartie. I don't want anyone to know. I want to keep it in the secret place of my heart, the part of me that still clings to hope.

3.

The Recorder Hall is dark and musty, like always. We've only been here a few times, to be honest. Lessons about the ship and its mission are given to every child, mad or not, at least once a year until their apprenticeship. It's vital that every person on *Godspeed* knows and understands the significance of what we're doing. We're carrying the hopes of an old planet across the universe in order to create a whole new world.

The entryway to the Recorder Hall is huge, with a tall

ceiling and tiny, narrow windows that are supposed to stream in light, but really just cast everything in shadows. Digital membrane screens stretch from floor to ceiling along the walls. We call them wall floppies, which is a stupid name, really, but they hang on the wall and they're, well, floppy. Each one glows now with an image—one shows a constellation, another a painting, another a sculpture.

We stand awkwardly in the center of the room, six teenagers surrounded by the history of both the old world and the ship. The nurse who escorted us slips out the door and closes it behind her, the sound a solid thud compared to the electronic doors of the Hospital that zip shut with a whisper.

"So . . ." Harley says, his voice ringing throughout the tall room despite his hushed tone. "This is boring."

Bartie, standing behind him, snorts with laughter. Victria rolls her eyes at them both, and Bartie silences immediately.

I turn away, my stomach twisting with envy. My eyes are drawn to clear hazel eyes—those of Luthor, the straggler of our group. He'd been watching me, staring at me, and he doesn't bother trying to hide his interest.

I blush and turn away.

"Thank you for coming out here today," a voice booms throughout the Recorder Hall. A man emerges from the other end of the entry way. He's very tall, with long, unkempt hair that almost covers a spider web scar on the side of his neck.

"Like we had a choice," Victria mumbles.

The man's head whips around. "You do," he says. "*You* always have a choice." He opens his mouth as if to say something more, but swallows the words. Instead, he says, "I am Orion, the Recorder."

"Why are you teaching us today?" Kayleigh asks. "Why not Doc?"

"Or one of the Shippers?" Bartie adds. "Are we not getting an apprenticeship?"

"Apprenticeships are for labor," Orion says. "You are not going to be laborers."

"Because we're loons," I can't help but say.

"Are you?" Orion asks sincerely. He blinks at me, as if trying to determine if I really am loons or not.

"I take the mental meds every day," I snap. I don't like the way he's looking at me.

"That's not a very good indication of whether or not you're crazy," Orion replies.

I start to snap something back, but Kayleigh's elbow jabs me in the ribs and I silence.

"The Recorder Hall is not just a record of knowledge and history," Orion says, sweeping his arms toward the wall floppies hanging from the ceiling. He crosses the room to the floppy labeled HISTORY. We all trot obediently behind him. The screen lights up as he swipes his hand across it, and a map of a peninsula and islands illuminates the screen.

"This is Greece, a country in Sol-Earth," Orion says.

My eyes slide to Kayleigh's. There's an intense sort of focus to her gaze, and no wonder. While the giant clay model of Sol-Earth hangs from ceiling of the entryway, its countries aren't labeled. We are taught that the world was divided into nations, but not the names of these divisions. The very fact that the old world was broken up into different countries proves why life aboard the ship is better. There's no point in learning the history of Sol-Earth's nations, except as a warning of bad civilizations we cannot let *Godspeed* emulate.

"The Greeks, they knew how to appreciate art," Orion continues. "They believed in art for art's sake, that a sculpture or a painting doesn't have a higher purpose—it just *is*."

A sinking sadness fills my chest. The ones in the Hospital who were better at math and science have been apprenticed because they have something to contribute to the ship. But us—me and Kayleigh and Victria and Bartie and Harley and Luthor—we're just artists. We have nothing to contribute.

"Or," Orion says, talking to the map in a contemplative tone, "perhaps it is better to say that art *is* a higher purpose in and of itself. That's what the Greeks understood—that's something even Eldest understands. Art is important. There is value in art that can't be tallied like the right or wrong answers on a test. Even here, even on this frexing ship, art is important."

Victria shifts uncomfortably beside me. No one speaks ill of *Godspeed* or its leaders, but Orion's dancing around contempt in a way that makes us all nervous. Except for Kayleigh. She's hanging on every word Orion says, her eyes glistening.

"Your assignment is to research the Greeks. They

made heroes of their artists—some they even made into 'gods.' Find a Greek that matches your artistic style."

I try to imagine it for a moment, a world that values people who sing. I've never been able to think of my singing as anything more than a worthless, throw-away skill.

Harley clears his throat. "I don't understand."

"Your parents are weavers, right?" Orion asks.

Harley nods. His usual carefree attitude is immediately hidden behind an emotionless mask: He doesn't like to talk about his parents. None of us do. Moving to the Hospital means leaving behind your parents. But if Harley's parents were like mine, it's not like they cared when he left. Or even noticed.

"In Greece," Orion continues as if nothing's different, "the best weaver in their history was a woman named Arachne. She was so good that the gods were jealous, and they turned her into a spider so she could only weave webs." My eyes drift down Orion's neck, to the spider web scar behind his left ear. He notices my glance and touches the scar before catching himself and lowering his hand.

"And what?" Bartie asks. "You want us to write a report on her, or whatever god matches our skills?"

"No," Orion says eagerly. "I want you to *create*. If, for example, you chose Arachne, then I want you to weave her story into a tapestry."

I can see the moment when understanding washes over each of our faces—he wants us to *make* art. A sloppy grin spreads over Harley's face. Luthor mutters to himself, as if coming up with ideas of what he'd like to do already. Even Victria looks ecstatic.

Godspeed isn't Greece: No matter what Orion says, it doesn't feel as if art is very much valued here. Doc has had us *research* art, sure, but never really experiment with it. He was much more focused on what our art could do *for* the ship, how we could turn it into something *useful*.

I catch Bartie's eye. Doc has never been able to give us assignments that use our talents. He could have Luthor make scale models out of clay instead of sculpting, or Harley can draw architectural plans instead of painting, but there wasn't much he could do with Bartie's skill with instruments or my singing voice.

"Your assignment," Orion repeats, "is to research art . . . and then *make* some."

It is a delicious challenge.

4.

"This is brilly," Harley says as we sit in a circle on the floor in the entryway of the Recorder Hall. We each have our own personal floppies, each flashing with images from ancient Greece. Orion ventured further into the Recorder Hall with promises to show us *real* books from Sol-Earth.

"I know!" Kayleigh says. She's so excited she's forgotten that she wants to be aloof in front of Harley. "I can't believe he's encouraging us to do art!"

Harley lights up at the joy in Kayleigh's voice. "What are you going to research?" he asks, leaning closer to

Kayleigh while she lets him. "I think you could be Poseidon." He holds his floppy out to her.

Kayleigh scans the information on this Greek "god." It seems ridiculous that the Greeks actually *worshipped* these people, thinking they had any kind of real power. Silly Sol-Earth fairytales and religions.

"Ew," Kayleigh tosses the floppy back to Harley. "This man is half-naked."

Harley laughs. "Yeah, but he's the god of the ocean, and you love to swim."

"Maybe you should study Aphrodite," Kayleigh says in a sticky-sweet voice, "and dress up in some seashells."

"I'm not a flirt," Harley says so seriously that the entire room silences. "Not with anyone but you."

Kayleigh blushes furiously and gets up to sit on the other side of Victria, putting me beside Harley instead.

Harley doesn't seem to mind. Maybe he's confident; maybe he just doesn't see a point in pretending to have any other feelings than those he holds for Kayleigh. He turns to me next, as if nothing's happened. "What about you? You could be a Siren."

I tap the word into my floppy and am greeted with an image of something that looks like a cross between a girl and a fish. "This looks more like something Kayleigh would like," I say. She *is* the one who spends every morning swimming in the pond behind the Hospital.

"No, read," Harley insists.

I start reading, the sounds of everyone else's gentle arguments disappearing as I focus on the story. I see now why Harley thought this particular mythological creature suited me: the Sirens sing too. My fingers trail along a portrait of a Siren perched on a rock, a stringed instrument in one hand as she stares impassively at the boy drowning in the water below her.

Yes. I like these Sirens.

By the time I look up, Orion's returned with the books. Harley flips through the pages too quickly, careless with the ancient paper made from real trees from Sol-Earth. We don't have trees on *Godspeed,* and we hardly ever use the synthetic paper made by the Shippers—everything's recorded on floppies instead. Orion scowls at Harley until he sets the book gently down on the ground.

"Have you selected your topic?" Luthor asks.

I nod and hold out the floppy to him. He smiles as he reads about the creatures that sing to lure men's ships to dangerous waters and sure death.

Harley glances up as Bartie leans over to read too. "Ha! Your voice could make men suicidal!" He crows with laughter, but I snatch the floppy out of his hands and read about the Greek that he selected. I know he didn't mean the words to sting, but they do.

"*Your* music is so bad Hades would keep you in the underworld to save us all from having to hear it!" I try to keep my voice light like his, turning the words into a harmless joke among friends. Nothing more than friends.

"It is not!" Bartie snatches the floppy away. "Orpheus was the greatest musician *of all time.*"

"Bet he couldn't sing," I snap back.

"Who have you all chosen?" Orion's voice calls out over our argument.

"Sappho," Victria says.

Harley snorts. "You *would* pick her."

"What's that supposed to mean?"

"I can't decide between Hephaestus and Prometheus," Kayleigh says, drawing attention to her. Victria shoots her a small smile.

"Why Prometheus?" Orion asks.

Harley taps the name into his floppy. "You don't want him. He gets his liver eaten out by a giant bird!"

"But I like the way he brought knowledge to people," Kayleigh says.

"But you're more of an inventor." Orion lifts the floppy out of her hands and swipes the screen, bringing up an image of a huge, ugly man with a forge behind him. "Hephaestus is probably more appropriate. And less dangerous."

Even here, we have to remind ourselves that Eldest is more of a god than any of these long-dead Greeks, and he can do much worse that have our livers ripped out.

"I'm selecting Pygmalion," Luthor says.

I jump a little; I'd forgotten how close he was to me. He's so *quiet*.

"Piggy, piggy!" Barite taunts. "That sounds about right!"

"Pygmalion was a sculptor," Orion says. "Good choice, Luthor. What about you, Harley?"

"I can't find any painters," he grumbles.

"Why don't you do a fresco—it's like painting, but with plaster—and you can use the Muses as your subject?" Orion suggests.

He bends down to show Harley the Muses, but I'm

distracted by Victria. She mouths something to me, indicating Bartie and Luthor with her head.

"What?" I mouth back.

Her eyes widen at me, and she jerks her head to Luthor. Then she glances significantly at Kayleigh, who's leaned in close to Harley, and jerks her head back.

"She wants us to give them some privacy," Luthor whispers in my ear.

"I—oh!" I say, blushing.

Victria rolls her eyes.

Scooping up the floppy and one of the books, I follow Victria and Bartie further into the Recorder Hall, passing closed doors leading to rooms full of books and Sol-Earth artifacts. Luthor trails behind me, chuckling at how Harley and Kayleigh remain ignorant of our plot.

Victria pauses at the door to the entry way. "I'll distract Orion in a minute, give them some real alone time." When I don't move, she adds, "You go on," and waves her hands at me.

I head further down the dark hallway. Luthor hesitates, then follows me, but Bartie winks and drops back to stay with Victria. I'm disappointed—I would actually like to talk to him about maybe working together on our project. He could compose music and I could write lyrics and maybe we could . . .

But he'd rather stay with Victria.

Fine.

Whatever.

I don't care.

"Let's go upstairs," Luthor says softly, so I follow him.

I've never explored the Recorder Hall this much before; I know that the second and third stories hold relics from Sol-Earth, but not much else.

Luthor leads me to a room on the second floor—a huge gallery with double doors. Unlike the entryway, this room is filled with light, illuminating the objects inside.

"What is this?" I whisper. Canvases hang from the walls, illuminated by the windows. Sculptures dot the tiled floor; a mobile made of glittering glass hangs from the ceiling.

"It's the art from past gens," Luthor says. He steps inside, and while I just stand there, gazing around, he watches my expression as if eager to see if he's pleased me.

"I . . . I didn't know," I say, awed. And I didn't. It's not that the Recorder Hall is banned or kept hidden—although you do have to have permission to see the books. It's that it never occurred to me that a ship led by Eldest could hold such treasures.

"And look," Luthor says, stepping over to the wall, where an electronic box is embedded. He adjusts a dial, and music drifts through the room.

"These were all made by people who lived on this ship," he says.

I close my eyes and *listen.*

The singer is a soprano, like me, and her voice is clear and rich. She sings about impossibilities: stars within reach, solid earth at her feet, and ocean mist kissing her cheeks.

When the song fades to static, I open my eyes.

Luthor's motionless, staring at me with a look on his face that I don't recognize. "Let's make this our studio," he says suddenly. "You and me. Let's work on our projects here." He pauses, wetting his lips. "Together."

I think about the adoration Harley showers on Kayleigh, the way Kayleigh's mouth twitches whenever he tries to snatch her hand in his. I think of the way Bartie hung back to stay with Victria.

"Yes," I say, and in that moment, nothing exists beyond him and me and the lingering strains of the music that hang between us.

5.

Orion gave us a whole month to complete our projects, but we waste no time getting started. An opportunity to dedicate our days to the arts we love has been rare in the Hospital, and none of us is taking that that time for granted. Kayleigh works outside—she's using metal and a blowtorch to make . . . *something*, but only she knows what. Harley has decided that he needs to work outside too, to keep his fresco wet, and the two of them have set up spaces near the koi pond Kayleigh likes to swim in.

Bartie tags along wherever Victria goes, and Victria wanders through the fields and to the City, scribbling in the little leather-bound book that Orion gave her after she told him her idea for a collection of poetry. It almost seems as if Bartie's taking his assignment too literally—he's following the object of his affection blindly no matter where she leads him. Still, I suspect Bartie would be devastated to discover what her notebook actually contains—my guess is that more than half her poems are in fact dedicated to Orion.

And Luthor and I? We meet each other every morning, before the solar lamp clicks on, and sneak into our little makeshift studio together.

"I'm glad you didn't decide to work with Bartie," he says after the first week.

"Why would I work with Bartie?" I ask innocently, even though that's what I'd thought I wanted before. I focus on typing notes on my floppy so he doesn't notice my blush.

Luthor smirks at me and turns his attention back to his own floppy. Orion has ordered clay for him, manufactured chemically in the labs on the Shipper Level, but when it arrives, he'll have to work quickly to finish his sculpture before it dries out. For that reason, Orion's insisted that he come up with a design before he actually starts sculpting.

"Seriously, Luthor," I say, "I'm really glad we're working together."

He mumbles something.

"What?" I ask.

"Luthe. You could call me Luthe. My friends do."

I wonder whom he means by "friends." Bartie? Probably, even though if you asked Bartie, I'm sure he wouldn't have applied the term "friend" to Luthor. Luthor has been living at the Hospital as long as anyone—in fact, I think he was one of the first Doc selected to move in. Even so, he's always been stand-offish at best.

I shoot him a quick smile. "I'm glad to be your friend,"

I say. "Would it be okay if I still call you Luthor, though? It —suits you."

He turns back to his floppy, but he can't hide his smile.

———

At the end of the second week, Victria taps on my bedroom door. It zips open before I have a chance to get up from my desk and answer her knock.

"Don't just come in!" I say, jumping up.

Victria rolls her eyes and plops down on my unmade bed.

There are no locks on *Godspeed*. We don't need them. The ship is so small that everyone respects privacy. On Sol-Earth, people had to worry about things like theft, but not here. *Godspeed* is perfectly safe.

Except from Victria when she wants to talk.

"Seleeeeene," she draws out my name.

"Whaaaat?" I mimic her whine.

She crashes into my pillows dramatically. "I'm bored."

I shove aside the sheet music I'd been working on. "Where's Kayleigh?" I ask.

"With Harley." Her voice drips with disdain, as if even his name disgusts her.

I glance to the window. "It's nearly time for the solar lamp to go dark. They're still working on their projects?"

Victria props herself up on her elbows. "I am *certain* that the one thing they're *not* doing is working on their projects."

I let her words sink in. "Oh!"

"Yeah."

"Well . . ." I pause, careful about which words I use. "What about you and, uh, Bartie?"

"He's annoying," she snaps, sitting up and tossing my pillow up in the air. She catches it, then stares at me. "What about you and Luthor?"

I shrug, not meeting her eyes.

"You've been working with him in the Recorder Hall a lot," she adds, leaning forward.

"Yeah, but . . ."

"Listen, be careful with him." She doesn't meet my eyes; her whole demeanor has changed. She sets the pillow back on my bed, carefully smoothing it out and pretending like the simple task deserves her full focus.

"Luthor's harmless." Even as I say it, I can hear the doubt in my own voice, the question seeking confirmation.

"He's . . . *creepy*," Victria says. "I just . . . I worry."

"You don't have to worry about me," I say as I shove her off my bed. "It's Kayleigh you should keep your eye on!"

But the concern wrinkling Victria's brow doesn't fade as she leaves.

———

Someone knocks on my door before the solar lamp clicks on the next day. "Who is it?" I call, yawning. I pull my cotton tank top over the waist of my soft knit shorts and stagger blearily to the door. At least I know it's not Victria; she'd have just barreled in before I had a chance to get up.

Luthor's waiting on the other side, looking excited.

"I know what I want to sculpt," he says, stepping into the room.

"What?" After the door zips closed behind him, I push the large button in my wall and soon the room is filled with the scent of breakfast. Wall food isn't that great—we could go to the caf instead and get something a little better—but it is convenient. I pull out the warm meat pasty from the cavity built into my wall and break it apart, offering half to Luthor.

He takes it, a flicker of surprise on his face. "Thanks," he mumbles.

"So," I say, spraying bread crumbs before I think to swallow. "What're you going to make?"

"You."

"What?"

"*You.*" Luthor sets his half of breakfast down on the desk. He's too excited; he needs both hands to fly around as he speaks. "I read more about the Pig-guy."

"Pygmalion," I say, smiling. I know the name better than he does.

"Yeah. And he made a sculpture of what he thought the ideal woman would be like. That's the whole point of his story, that he created this perfect woman with his art. And that's what I want to do. I want to make the perfect woman."

"And you want . . . *me?*"

Luthor pauses in his flurried excitement, really looking at me, taking in my disheveled hair, wrinkled clothes, and sleep-encrusted eyes. "Of course you," he says simply, and my heart fills with song.

———

I stand perfectly still in our little studio as Luthor sketches me. He wants to make the statue in a "classical" pose, as he says it, and he keeps telling me to rearrange my arms, or hunch my back more, or hold up one hand.

"No, no, no," he says, frustrated. I'm not offended—he's frustrated with my posing in the same way that I get frustrated with my voice when I can't reach a note. "Like this."

He strides across the floor and pulls my arms down. He runs both his hands down my arms, making my elbows straighten and pulling my hands slightly behind my hips. I glance down at him; he doesn't see me as a person in this moment—I'm not Selene, I'm a model.

Luthor slips behind me, pushing one hand into my spine so my back curves inward, making my chest jut forward.

Slowly, he walks around, inspecting me and my pose, stopping when he faces me. "Up," he says gently, tapping my chin. I lift my face toward the ceiling, the warm light from the high windows cascading down my cheeks.

"Perfect," he whispers. "You're perfect."

I glance down at him, careful not to move my body or my face. When he looks at me now, I know he's seeing past my skin, into the very heart of who I am.

———

Orion approves Luthor's design quickly, and if he thought there was something odd about his selection of me as a model, he doesn't say anything. After lunch, workers from the Feeder Level bring a huge pillar of brown clay, and Luthor tells them to drop it right there, in the center of the floor, where the light from the windows hits it just right.

He brings in buckets of water and lays out his tools in a neat arc next to the clay.

"We could go down to the pond with Kayleigh and Harley," I suggest.

Luthor shakes his head, his attention focused on lining up each tool correctly. They look almost like Doc's medical instruments: a dull-bladed knife, tiny needlelike picks, a scalpel.

"I want to work *here*," Luthor says. "With you. Alone."

As if on cue, Victria barges into the studio. "So," she says loudly, her voice bouncing off the walls, "this is where you two have been hiding."

Bartie trails behind Victria. He carries his guitar on a strap across his shoulders, one hand unconsciously stroking the strings.

"We're *working*," Luthor says pointedly.

"So are we. Looking for inspiration and all that." Victria ignores him and heads straight over to me. There's something almost protective in her stance.

"Look for inspiration somewhere else," Luthor growls, and I can't blame him. He was *just* about to get started on the sculpture he's planned for two weeks; Victria and Bartie's interruption could not have come at a worse time.

"I need Selene." Victria lifts one shoulder, as if she's helpless in the face of her whimsical muse.

"So do I." Luthor hasn't moved away from his clay, but his hands are motionless, his body stiff.

Victria leans over. "You've got a sketch." Her words are casual, but she touches my arm, pressing into my skin as if trying to convey a message to me through my flesh. Bartie shifts nervously by the door.

"But I'll still need *her*."

Before the two of them can dissolve into a real fight, I speak up. "Why do you need me, Victria?"

"I need a song. Music."

"You have Bartie." I hope none of the others notice the bitterness in my voice. She does have Bartie, all of him, even if she doesn't appear to want him the way I used to.

"But I need singing."

"Yeah," Bartie says, looking up for the first time. "You're the Siren, remember. Sing us a song that'll make us want to drown."

Victria and Bartie chuckle at the jab, but Luthor just scowls. "Will you leave if she sings?" he says.

Victria hesitates, but Bartie says, "Yes."

"Just get rid of them," Luthor says, waving his hand as if he's sacrificing something to let me sing.

"I . . . I don't know what to sing," I say, suddenly shy.

"Sing one of the songs you've been working on for Orion's project."

My hand moves unconsciously to the loose papers scattered on my makeshift desk. "They're not ready."

Victria rolls her eyes. "Just sing."

———

And so I sing.

I start with a long note—a high E—and I hold it as long as I can, letting the strength of my voice lift the sound to the ceiling. I tilt my head back and shut my eyes, letting myself forget about Luthor and whatever it is about him that makes Victria nervous, forget about the way Bartie's presence fills me with regret, forget everything but the sound.

I hold the note until my breath gives out, and I collapse a little on myself as I suck in more air, but I don't open my eyes.

I know the notes I want, the words that will go with them.

I start softly, a contrast to the opening of the song.

I sing of being afraid, and of finding friendship. Of love and longing.

Very softly, Bartie picks up the tune, adding simple chords in key with my voice. His guitar sounds hesitant at first, but as my voice rises, the chords grow stronger. My voice falters a bit, a little sad at the way we can make such beautiful music together, despite the fact that Bartie will never love me the way I had wanted him to. Then I glance at Luthor, and my song surges in my throat.

I sing about the ocean I've never seen in real life. I sing about loneliness. I make the Siren into something sympathetic. She doesn't mean to kill what she loves. She just can't help it.

Silence wraps around me, and I fill it with my voice. I sing of everything that's wrong, and everything that's right, of hope and death. I sing of infinite wonder, of how every-thing must end.

When I open my eyes, my chest is heaving, my head thrown back, my arms cast behind me. I've unconsciously formed myself into Luthor's Pygmalion tribute. And even though I sang a love song, my eyes go not to Bartie, who stills his guitar string with one shaking hand, but to Luthor, who's snatched up his notebook and is resketching me, trying to capture the moment of my singing onto paper so he can carve it out of clay.

"Thanks," Victria whispers.

"Was that what you were looking for?" I ask. There's a sheen of sweat on my brow.

"Yeah," she says slowly.

"I'm not finished." I'm suddenly self conscious, aware of the way my voice cracked in the second verse, the clut-tered lyrics I rushed through in the third. "I mean, I'm still working on the lyrics and the rhythm."

"It's good."

"It's really sad," Bartie says.

I laugh. "It's not sad! It's a love song!"

Bartie stands, slinging his guitar onto his back. "Love songs can still be sad."

"Come on," Victria says, putting one hand on Bartie's elbow. "Let's leave these two alone to work."

She nods to me as she leaves, and although she still sidesteps around Luthor and avoids his gaze, there must have been something in my song to make her know that he's no threat and that our greatest focus now is on our art.

As if to prove it, Luthor picks up a long-bladed tool and

starts to saw at the clay. "I've got the perfect idea," he says without stopping. "I know exactly how to make this work." He glances up at me now. "But—would you mind singing while I sculpt? You could practice some more for your presentation."

I'd intended to present Orion with a series of songs, an entire opera, but I only had pieces of each song done here and there. I hated to start singing something incomplete; the love song was bad enough, but at least it was mostly done.

Still, there's something in the way Luthor's hands slide over the clay, in the silence of his work, that makes me want to fill the studio with music once more.

I open my mouth and sing.

———

Luthor works fast, not breaking for meals. The clay Orion ordered is chemically produced not to dry completely until Luthor applies a glaze to the outside, but the more he handles it, the more difficult it is to work with, becoming less pliable and more prone to crumbling.

I don't even think about leaving. How could I? Still, my voice cracks and, despite drinking copious amounts of water, I slowly succumb to silence. I've done more work on my songs today than on any day of the previous two weeks, and I know that a large part of that is because Luthor's infectious need to sculpt has influenced my need to sing.

The gallery's overhead lights click on when the solar

lamp clicks off. Luthor growls at the change in light, but barely pauses.

I move behind him, inspecting the work he's done.

The sculpture is beautiful, far more beautiful than me. The clay version of me is smooth and lithe, more graceful in her stillness than I could ever be when I move.

"Can you—" he starts, then gets distracted by his sculpture, smoothing down a ridge in the clay. I watch as his hands run over the surface. He must be nearly finished— the sculpture looks so real now, as if this perfect earthen copy of me will lift her feet up and step from the narrow base.

Luthor's hands move to her forehead, four fingers on each hand swirling across the sculpture's brow, over her closed, delicate eyelids, along her cheeks, down the hollows of her neck, straining with a silent song, lingering on her collarbone and trailing, finally, finally, coming to rest on her clay breasts.

I take a shaky breath.

"I like to make the lines smooth," Luthor says, his attention still on his sculpture. "Everything has to blend together."

"It's beautiful," I say, my voice softer than I'd intended.

He pauses now, and turns to look at me. "You're beautiful," he says.

He lifts his mud-coated hands toward me, then stops. I lean forward. He touches me on my forehead, just as he touched his sculpture, and I close my eyes, pressing my face into his hand. I ignore the clay he leaves on my skin, relishing the feel of his gentle finger trailing over my face, down my neck, across my collarbone . . . but he stops. I open my eyes.

He pulls me closer to him.

And the kiss we share makes me glad that I'm not just an empty, clay girl.

6.

I don't go back to the Hospital until well after dark, and when I do, I leave Luthor in our studio. He's still working like mad on the sculpture, even though, to me, it looks complete.

I wander down the path between the Recorder Hall and the Hospital. I've spent half my life in love with Bartie, who never really noticed me, and now here's Luthor, who I'd never really seen before, and there's this thing between us that I'll never be able to ignore again.

Near the pond, a huge monstrosity grows up from the ground. Kayleigh's work—a mobile metal sculpture that looks half organic, half nightmare. She's used some sort of reddish-clear gel to create the appearance of fire at the base, and added groping metal arms reaching through the flames, up to the sky. But our sky is made of metal too, and if this sculpture is grasping for freedom, it will just meet another wall.

Harley's fresco looks like nothing but a plaster sheet—I suspect he's been busier looking at Kayleigh than doing any work. He usually paints every day, but he's been rather distracted by the fact that Kayleigh's no longer turning him away.

I'm in a silent, contemplative mood by the time I make it back to the Hospital.

"Hey, Selene!"

I jump, surprised by the sudden voice.

"I've been waiting for you," Bartie says, smiling up from the comfy couch in the common room. A trill of music follows his words; his guitar lies on his lap, his fingers unconsciously strumming the strings.

I cross the room and sit in the chair opposite him. A month ago, finding out that Bartie had been waiting up just to see me would have made my face flush and my knees shake. But now, I can still feel Luthor's kiss on my lips.

"Why?" I ask simply.

"Victria . . ." His voice trails off.

This would be the point, a month ago, that would have made me want to cry. But the part of my heart that will always recognize that Bartie was my first love is silent.

"I'm sure she'll come around," I say. "Victria's not a very, I don't know, *emotional* person. But I bet she'll fall for you eventually."

Bartie laughs. "No, that's not what I meant!" Still, he's pleased with what I said.

"Then what?"

Bartie shifts uncomfortably, his hand going back to his guitar, running his fingers up and down the strings. "Victria said you . . . and Luthe . . ."

"It's *fine*," I say immediately. Better than fine.

"Luthe . . . he's not . . ." Bartie shifts again, glancing out the dark window. "He's said things . . . I just . . ."

"Victria should pay more attention to her love life and less to mine," I snap.

"Listen," Bartie says, leaning closer. "If Luthe has friends, then I'm one. And the way he talks about people . . . about girls . . ."

"Girls? More than one?" I ask, my heart plunging.

"That's not what I'm trying to say."

I can't help but let a sigh of relief escape my lips.

"Just be careful, okay?" Bartie finally mumbles.

I nod, but I'm still not sure what he means.

Bartie's hands drift back to his guitar. "Want to jam a bit?"

"Jam?" I laugh.

"I read about it. It's what they used to call making music, back on Sol-Earth."

"*Jam.*" I say again. Such a ridiculous word.

"I've been working a bit on this," Bartie adds, and he lifts the guitar up into its proper position, his calloused fingers pressing into the strings on the neck. He fumbles, listening to the chords, until he finds the right harmony.

The song is fast, and gets louder as he goes, but it still sounds melancholy to me. I think it's the way that the notes weave in and out, always going back to the same deep, resonating chords, as if, no matter how quickly Bartie's fingers dance on the strings, he can't help but fall into the same sad melody.

When he glances up at me, he stops the song abruptly.

"What is it?" I ask as the music dies.

"You looked as if you were going to cry," he says.

I touch my cheek, but it's dry.

"How about this instead?" Bartie says, smiling, and he starts up on the same melody he'd made to match the song I wrote.

I smile, and as soon as I catch the rhythm, I open my mouth to sing. I don't let the music rip from me as I did in the studio before; instead I force the song to stream from me like a steady flow of quiet water. I don't want to wake anyone up, and even if the common room is separated from the rest of the Hospital, it's not soundproof.

Still, the music overwhelms me. By the time I'm at the end, my voice is raised, and I am breathless.

And it's not until then that I notice Luthor, standing in front of the elevator, watching me.

Bartie presses his palm into the guitar strings, silencing them. Luthor doesn't make a sound as his eyes dart from Bartie to me and back again. I'm suddenly aware of how close I am to Bartie, of the flush on my cheeks, of the way my fingers are almost touching his knee. I snatch my hand back.

Luthor walks out of the common room without saying a word.

———

When I wake up the next morning, my door is open. I know I closed it the night before, but it's open now, light from the hallway streaming inside. I get up, rubbing my eyes and pulling my tank top down over my hips as I press the button to zip the door closed. I wonder if it was Victria, come to talk or barge in as usual, and if at the last minute she decided to let me sleep. Or maybe it was just a door malfunction.

I press the button on my wall for food delivery, and while I wait, I stick my fingers into the small cavity by the door. A small blue-and-white pill waits for me there. I stare at the capsule, wondering at how this tiny pill separates me from nearly everyone else on the ship outside the Hospital.

I swallow the pill dry. Doc says we're loons, that our restlessness and artistic expression comes from this insanity, and that the Inhibitor pills are the only thing that keeps us from really losing it.

But I think Kayleigh is probably right. The Inhibitor pills don't keep us from cracking; they keep us human, they keep us from turning into the passive nothingness the rest of the Feeders feel.

The little compartment in my wall opens, and steam wafts out of it, leaving behind the scent of a meat pasty. I gobble it up as quickly as I can; wall food isn't the best, and it's unbearable to eat cold.

I must have overslept—no one's around the common room, and the Hospital is empty. I head straight to the Recorder Hall. Orion nods at me in the entryway, but is busy working on a floppy.

Something blocks the door of our little studio, and I have to push hard to get inside.

The first thing I notice is Luthor. He's brown with clay, covered up to his elbows, with splotches of it decorating his clothes and great swaths over his brow. Little lines of sweat trickle through the dirt on his face.

Underneath the clay and sweat is a scowl angrier than any I've seen..

The next thing I notice is the sculpture. While Luthor's face radiates with emotion, the clay face of the sculpture is blank. No wonder Luthor's hands are caked with mud. He's smoothed every feature from the sculpture's visage, making the cheeks so flat that they're almost gone, smoothing the nose into nothing but a bump, completely erasing the lips. The eyes—he'd worked a solid day on the eyes alone, using a tiny pick-like tool to carve in eyelashes—are now nothing more than slight indentations under the barely-there brow.

There is an eerie quality to the sculpture now: The body is still intact, perfectly beautiful and meticulously detailed, but the face is nothing but a flat shadow.

Still, it seems to stare at me with its nothing eyes.

"It's better now," Luthor says flatly.

"It was lovely before." My voice comes out weak.

Luthor levels his glare at me. "It's better now," he repeats.

My hand reaches behind me for the door, my body seeking an escape before my mind can tell me what I need to do.

"What were you doing with Bartie?" Luthor asks.

"What?"

"Last night. In the common room. What were you doing with Bartie?" He bites off each word as if it tastes foul in his mouth.

"Nothing. Singing. Nothing."

Luthor reaches toward me with his clay-covered hands.

I flinch. He notices, and, rather than becoming gentler as he would have a day before, his hand tenses and his eyes narrow. He touches my brow, his fingers raking across my skin forcefully as he drags them down, over my eyelids, leaving brown streaks on my face.

"You're mine," he whispers. "*Mine.*"

I get the frex out of there.

7.

From that point on, I don't work in the studio. I go at night —with Bartie and Victria, both wearing looks of concern and worry—to get my notebooks and sheet music from the Hall. Luthor's covered his sculpture up with a large cloth, and I don't have the courage to look at the blank face again.

My music takes on a different tone as I write with Victria and Bartie, who've turned the garden behind the Hospital into their studio. It's nice to be able to get help from a poet when I work on lyrics, or advice from a fellow musician when I'm struggling to find chords. I work quicker—but at the same time, it feels as if I've lost some of the emotion behind the music. I'd started out writing love songs, and ended up writing sad ones. Perhaps appropriate for the Sirens, but not for me.

And then, almost before I've really had a chance to put everything together the way I want, it's time to present our work to Orion.

Kayleigh and Harley enlist all of our help to get their pieces from the pond behind the Hospital up to the Recorder Hall. Harley wanted to do the presentations by the pond, but Orion insisted they be done inside the Hall. Besides, the projects are supposed to be installed in the galleries on the upper floors once we're done with our presentations. I assume that means Luthor had to clean up as well, that our studio is once more just the gallery, but I try not to think on it too much.

The gallery seems darker with three hulking new additions—Kayleigh's metal sculpture, Harley's fresco, and Luthor's covered-up clay sculpture.

Orion asks us each to explain our work as part of our presentations. Kayleigh goes first, followed by Harley, but I barely hear them. I'm too busy staring at the bumpy cloth over Luthor's sculpture. It doesn't have that same familiar shape I'd come to know. It seems shorter.

Orion nods to Luthor, indicating that he should go next, but Luthor shakes his head. Instead, Victria begins reciting her poetry.

It's not until Bartie goes that I am able to draw my attention away from Luthor's too-short sculpture.

His music is hollow in the best possible way. It speaks of longing and sorrow, and I want to fill it with my voice, but I don't. It's better this way.

As his music fades, I step forward with my own. I close my eyes and forget about everything and just sing.

And for that short moment, everything is right.

But then the moment disappears.

I open my eyes, and I'm still here. And so is Luthor.

"Thank you, Selene," Orion says. "Now, it's your turn, Luthor."

He doesn't bother introducing his work. Instead,

Luthor steps up to his sculpture and in one swift motion rips the cloth off.

I gasp—the only sound in the silent gallery.

The sculpture is no longer faceless—it's headless. From the rough marks at the decimated remains of the neck, I can easily imagine him wrapping his fingers around the clay, carefully and precisely squeezing, squeezing, *squeezing* until the head simply popped right off.

From the neck down, the sculpture is beautiful—even more graceful and elegant than I'd remembered. There are cuticles etched in the fingernails, veins at the delicate wrists. Individual toes curl around the base, and the draping gown looks as if it is made of silk, not mud.

But from the neck up—nothing.

"Well." Orion's voice cuts through the ringing silence. "This is quite . . . illuminating, Luthor."

Luthor lets the sheet that had been covering his sculpture drop to the floor as he turns and storms out of the gallery.

———

Even Kayleigh and Harley, as wrapped up as they are in each other, have noticed the way Bartie and Victria never leave my side. Their worry is palpable.

"Go to Doc," Harley finally says. "Ripping the head off a sculpture of someone is loons. Maybe he can up Luthor's meds."

"I don't think the meds we take have anything to do with being loons," Kayleigh says. "They just—"

"This isn't the time for that," Victria snaps. I'm surprised; I've never seen her be short with Kayleigh before. "But Harley's right. We should talk to Doc. Or maybe even Eldest?"

We let the weight of her words sink in before I say anything. "Not Eldest. It's just a creepy sculpture. No reason to contact Eldest."

Although no one says anything, the tension in the room dissolves a bit now that I've said to leave Eldest out of it.

"Still—Doc?" Bartie says.

I shake my head. "It's just a sculpture."

———

I can't sleep that night, which is why, when my door zips open, I'm awake to see Luthor standing in the doorway.

"You were supposed to be asleep," he says.

"You're supposed to be in your own room," I snap back.

He shrugs and steps inside, letting the door zip closed behind him.

"I didn't say you could come in!"

He just stands there.

"Get out!" I say, my voice rising.

In two steps, he's at my bed, his open hand covering my mouth. I try to shout, but the sound is muffled. He presses his weight against me, pushing me into my mattress. I thrash around, but can't escape his grip.

"You were supposed to be *mine*," he says. His breath is hot, his pupils dilated.

I shake my head the best I can under his grip.

"I don't like to *share*."

His hand slips down. "I don't know what you're talking about!" I yell.

But his hand isn't letting me go—it's just moving further down. His other hand joins the first around my neck.

I am hyperaware of the situation. I can feel each heavy thud of my heart growing stronger and faster. I can feel each of his fingers around my throat, each pressing into my skin. He's not choking me; he's just making sure I know that he *could*.

Unbidden and unwanted, an image of his sculpture comes into my mind: a perfect body with its head squeezed off.

My eyes burn. "Don't," I whisper, afraid to say more. The word has to fight its way up my throat to my mouth.

"I *could*," he says. "I could. I can do whatever I want."

"Don't," I plead.

"You sing. You become someone else when you sing— more beautiful, more perfect."

His index finger strokes the front of my throat, where my vocal chords are.

"Don't sing for anyone else," he orders.

I nod my head—anything to make him go away.

His grip tightens around my neck, pushing me further into my mattress. He lifts his right leg, and, without removing his hands from my throat, he climbs over me so that he's straddling me in my own bed.

His full weight presses down against me.

Tears leak from my eyes, dripping into my hair.

"You're *mine*," he whispers.

———

It is a very long time before he leaves, but when he finally does, a part of me has already died.

———

My back is uncomfortably straight in the blue plastic chair across from Doc's desk in his office.

He steeples his fingers as he looks at me. "But," he says in a carefully controlled voice, "he didn't actually *do* anything?"

For answer, I remove the scarf around my neck. Ten long fingerprint-shaped bruises decorate my throat.

"But—nothing else?" Doc shifts uncomfortably. "He threatened you, yes, I understand that, but he didn't actually . . . ?"

"Would it matter if he did?" I ask. My voice is raspy, a mixture of the gasping sobs that raked through my throat in the shower this morning and the pressure Luthor exerted on my vocal chords as he—

Doc leans forward. "This is very serious," he says. "I think perhaps I should give Luthor some hormone suppressants, at least until the Season. . . ."

"Pills? You're just going to give him pills?"

"His, er, desire for you isn't entirely natural. We can tamp down that desire, at least for a few years, until the Season."

"I'm not just worried about his desire."

Doc's eyes drift lower, to the bruises on my neck.

"I could bring Eldest into this," he mutters, half to himself. "But the thing is . . ."

"What?" My feeble voice cracks. "What is it? Why are you trying to nicely say that Luthor won't be punished for what he's done to me?"

"But if he didn't actually do anything—"

"What do you want me to say?" I stand up, my voice straining against my desire to shout. "That he held me down on the bed, even when I begged him to get up? That he crushed my throat until I couldn't make a sound? That he *laughed* at me as I struggled against him?" That he did things to me that I'm too disgusted to even describe with words.

Doc won't meet my eyes.

"Luthor is skilled in tactile and kinetic studies," he tells his neatly ordered desk. "He may be focused on creating sculptures now, but his skills could lead to an advancement in modular studies of the ship's engines, or help increase efficiency in the City or through the floppy network. . . ."

"And all I can do is sing," I croak.

I collapse back in the chair, hoping for Doc to protest, but we both know it's true. There's not much room for art on *Godspeed*; I'm superfluous at best. People like Kayleigh or Luthor will be able to find a productive way to contribute to the ship. People like me or Bartie will be able to do nothing more than provide some amusement for the real workers.

Luthor's more important than me, because his skills

can aid the ship. A song is nothing compared to productivity.

I laugh, a bitter, cracked sound damaged by Luthor's chokehold on me last night.

I can't even sing, not now. One day—soon, if Doc's right—my vocal chords will heal.

But could I ever really sing again? If Luthor says I can only ever sing for him, and he can do whatever he wants on this ship that values people based on what labor or skills they can provide, dare I ever make music?

"I'll start Luthor on hormone suppressants," Doc says in the silence. "That should stop his . . . urges."

But not his hands, his big, strong hands that choked the sound out of me, that popped the head off his sculpture, that held the razor-sharp scalpels he used to carve into clay, that he could use to carve into me.

8.

"We'll protect you," Victria says. Kayleigh, sitting on my bed, nods her head. "If Doc won't protect you, we will."

"What can you do?" I ask with a feeble laugh.

Kayleigh and Victria exchange glances. "The boys will help," Kayleigh says. "Harley and Bartie."

"They don't know me that well."

"They'll still help."

I can see it now: a lifetime where I'm always watched by at least one of them. Before, I had thought of Kayleigh as a sometime friend and Victria as an occasional companion. Harley and Bartie were always in the background of my mind. But I know—I can see it in the earnest looks both girls are giving me—that here is a chance for me to become something more to them all.

Not friend. Ward.

"I can't ask that of you, of any of you," I say.

Victria shakes her head. "We can't let that happen to you again."

She looks at my neck, but she can't see the wounds I've hidden behind my clothes.

"You can't protect me all day, every day."

"You can move into my room," Kayleigh says.

"Or mine," Victria adds.

I stare out the window.

"Selene?" Kayleigh asks. Something in her voice draws my attention to her. "You forgot to take your pill," she says. She holds out the little blue-and-white capsule that holds the drugs that keep me conscious, aware of the world.

I hadn't forgotten it.

"Silly me," I mutter, taking the pill. Kayleigh watches me carefully as I put it on my tongue and pretend to swallow.

But I don't.

After a while, I plead a headache, and the two girls leave. They don't go far; I can hear them talking, guarding my room. They shout at Luthor when he gets too close; I can hear him denying their accusations, their voices raising until Doc comes out and silences everyone.

I spit the blue-and-white pill out of my mouth and into the toilet, then flush it away.

Kayleigh said the pills made you nothing, and nothing seems like a pretty good thing to be right now.

Someone knocks on my door. I know it can't be Luthor —he doesn't knock.

Doc stands on the other side. "I've sent your little guards to their rooms," he says. Then his harsh expression melts. "I've also posted a guard—a real guard—at Luthor's room. I don't want you to feel threatened."

But I do. Guard or no. Because eventually, in a few days or weeks or even a whole month, the guard will go away. And I still won't have a lock on my door. And Luthor won't have forgotten.

You can never escape from me. Those were the last words he said to me, just before he left my room that night.

But in the end, it's remarkably easy to escape.

As I walk past the common room, I can see the way things will one day be. Kayleigh is snuggled into Harley's arm on the couch by the window—their love will grow and spread and be everything they want. Bartie plays a song for Victria. Victria may or may not fall for the guitar player, but their friendship won't fade. They are an idyllic vision of what I once wanted in my life.

In the corner, watched closely by Doc, is Luthor. He stares at me, eyes narrowed, as I cross the room. He blames me for the close watch he's been under these past few weeks, the additional pills. He hasn't forgotten.

But I almost have.

I take the elevator down to the lobby, then stroll down the path that leads from the Hospital to the Recorder Hall. I think about going into the Hall, maybe seeing the sculpture one last time, but the idea doesn't create an urge in me to make the effort to continue up the stairs.

Orion stands in the doorway. He starts to talk to me, but then he frowns as I pass by.

The path bleeds into the road that leads deeper into the Feeder Level. I know where I'm going—I've already talked about this with Doc, who got permission from Eldest for my reassignment.

Kayleigh was right. Without the pills, you really do feel nothing.

And nothing can be nice.

———

I open my palm, letting my last blue-and-white pill drop heedlessly to the ground.

———

I stand at the fence, staring down at the large rabbits
     used for meat on the ship. This is my new job.

Not songs.

Rabbits.

I glance back once.

. . .

Luthor will forget about me. He wanted my music, but empty people don't sing. I'll stay here. I will care for the rabbits. I will let myself become a nothing, and then Luthor won't want me, because there will be nothing to want.

It took several days before I felt the fear fade.

I didn't know that everything else would fade too.

But it's nice to be without the fear. Without the sad.

In the end, it didn't seem like such a big price to pay.

My songs, in exchange for nothing.

Nothing is nice.

Empty is good.

. . .

I cross over the fence. The rabbits hop. Up and down. Ears twitch.

I will be this girl, the girl who cares for the rabbits. Luthor took my music when he took everything else from me that night. What does it matter to me if I let the emptiness fill my shell?

9. The Day I Die

I hum a song.

I do that sometimes.

Hum.

I like sounds.

"Hello, Selene," a deep male voice says from the fence of the rabbit fields.

I stop humming.

.   .   .

"Do you remember me?" the man asks.

"You're Luthor," I say.

Luthor nods. "I told you before, call me Luthe. All my friends do."

But . . . I don't think he is a friend.

The fence around the rabbit field is nothing but chicken wire. He crumples it and shoves it away as easily as if it were made of paper.

"Selene," he says. I like sounds, but I don't like the way my name snarls around his lips.

"You were always my perfect girl," he says softly. The rabbits scurry out of his way as he walks slowly toward me.

Runrunrunrunrunrunrunrunrun. My mind screams at me, but my body doesn't move.

. . .

Everything is dull around me. A splintered memory jabs into my brain, trying to spark life into me, but everything is slow and steady. I can hear my heartbeat in my ears, a dull, normal *beat . . . beat . . . beat*. Not the panicked racing of the rabbit's heartbeat when I hold it down. But I feel like a rabbit, one selected for slaughter.

Luthor touches the side of my face, runs his fingers down my cheek, tucks a strand of hair behind my ear.

"Sing for me," he says.

"Singing isn't productive," I say. But I do sing, sometimes. Or hum. I like sounds. The rabbits like sounds. Sometimes we sing together.

But I don't want to sing for him.

Luthor's hands slip down my neck, his fingers pressing slightly against my throat. "Sing," he commands.

My mouth opens, my body automatically ready to obey the command.

· · ·

But there is something inside me that silences my voice.

I will not give him what he wants, this rebel inside me whispers.

I do not sing.

Luthor's grip on my neck tightens, and he pushes me down, first to my knees, then to my back. "You are mine," he growls. "If I can't have her, I *will* take you."

My body doesn't protest. It has been trained by years of drugs and acquiescence.

I shut my eyes.

"You're more like clay now than you were before."

I open my eyes.

Luthor is grinning.

.   .   .

"In the story, Pygmalion turned his girl of clay into a human. But I have turned a human into a girl of clay. And that is, by far, the better option."

I open my mouth.

And I sing then. Not the song Luthor wants. I sing for myself, a dirge, a mournful wail. I sing—I scream—until Luthor's hands around my throat silence me.

And I die. But at least I die in song.

CONTINUE READING

Read on for a free sample of Beth's based on "The Turing Test," *The Body Electric*, **as well as notes about the inspiration for each of the previous stories.**

Never miss another story or book from Beth! Sign up for her newsletter at: http://bethrevis.com

If you are a classroom teacher or educational professional who would like to use a story from this collection for your students' educational use, please contact the author at authorbethrevis@gmail.com for information on classroom availability and sets.

DOCTOR-PATIENT CONFIDENTIALITY

The idea for this story came from watching an episode of *Doctor Who*—specifically the 2010 Christmas special entitled "A Christmas Carol." I wanted to play with the idea of an impossible situation, a love that was true but could not exist in proper time. It's also more my answer to *Romeo and Juliet*—a truly star-crossed love that doesn't give up.

Apparently, I quite like the name Thomas as well. Despite there being more than four years between this story and "The Most Precious Memory," Benny's name was originally Tommy, and was only changed for this collection.

THE MOST PRECIOUS MEMORY

This is the oldest story in the collection, although it is one of the most recently published. I wrote this story while I was teaching high school, well before I'd written *Across the Universe*. Keen readers will see the girl described as having "sunset hair," a feature I couldn't help but include in the novel to describe my main character Amy when I wrote her years later.

THE GIRL & THE MACHINE

After watching the movie *The Time Traveler's Wife*, I couldn't help but think it was a really, really fortunate thing that the main character, who could travel through time, wasn't a giant jerk. He's basically a decent guy, and when he slides through time (naked) and meets previous versions of the woman he's going to marry, he doesn't take advantage of the situation. Unfortunately for my characters, I couldn't help but wonder what would happen if someone who had far fewer morals had the power to travel through time. Great powers don't always go to the good guys.

The main character's name, Heather Gardner-Wells, is a nod to the original time traveler, H.G. Wells.

LAG

My husband told me about an old *Outer Limits* episode with a teleportation twist one evening. We were never able to find the episode again (so I've yet to see it), but I loved the idea of teleportation going...wrong. If I could have one piece of sci fi tech in the current world, I'd totally throw away hover cars for the chance of teleportation. Would the possible chance of dying and being reanimated as a clone prevent people from wanting to have near-instantaeous travel? I honestly don't know.

Longtime readers will know I have a deep love for *Firefly* and *Serenity*—when Kimiko mentions that they won't be able to stop the signal, I'm alluding to the same signal the Operative and the Alliance can't stop when Mal releases it to the 'verse.

THE TURING TEST

My husband and I were sitting in Subway one afternoon, discussing science and artificial intelligence, as one does. He mentioned the turing test in passing, and that led me down a rabbit-hole trail of research into Alan Turing's life and the idea of machines thinking for themselves. In one intense sitting, I'd written "The Turing Test." The main ideas I explored here stayed with me and eventually became my next novel, *The Body Electric.*

I slipped in several allusions in this story. Many characters are named in reference to Philip K. Dick's *Do Androids Dream of Electric Sheep?* Elektra Shepherd's name comes from the title, Dr. Richard K. Philip is an inversion of the author's name, and Andy is the nickname for androids in the novel (his last name, Deckard, is an allusion to the main character's name). The test subject identity number is ES42—42, of course, being the meaning to life, the universe, and everything, according to Douglas Adams and *The Hitchhiker's Guide to the Galaxy.* Rory

Rivers's name comes from Rory and River Song, characters in *Doctor Who*.

MALFUNCTION

"Malfunction" came about as a culmination of several events in recent history, mainly the on-going struggle for reproductive rights in America. A law that stripped women of safe abortion procedures if they were past six weeks pregnant prompted me to put my thoughts onto paper—too often, women aren't even aware they're pregnant by the time that law limited their rights. I wanted to show an extreme case of time constraints, but also portray the way such a personal medical situation can impact women in a society that utterly dismisses their health. So many women are not given proper time, funds, or care to become mothers, and they are only valued for their work.

AS THEY SLIP AWAY

This novella takes place in the world of *Across the Universe*, my first published novel. Fans of the Beatles may recognize that the line "as they slip away" is a part of the lyrics of the song "Across the Universe" by Paul McCartney and John Lennon.

Greek mythology and literature obviously played an important role in this story, and, in fact, Selene is named for the goddess of the moon. Kayleigh, however, is named for Kaylee from *Firefly*.

THE BODY ELECTRIC

Continue reading for a sample of *The Body Electric!* Written in the tradition of Philip K. Dick's *Blade Runner* and *Total Recall*, this young adult novel follows the story of Ella Shepherd as she discovers that her ability to enter other people's minds and alter their memories may not be entirely unique.

Chapter One

"Don't ever forget how much I love you," Dad says.

I dig my toes into the warm Mediterranean sand. The water is a perfect blue, speckled with the white foam of cresting waves. When I tilt my head back, I can feel the warmth of the sun, a gentle sea breeze lifting strands of my short, brown hair and blowing them into my face.

But none of this is real.

"It is real!" I shout.

Dad turns around, a look of surprise on his face. "What was that, Ella?" he asks.

"Nothing," I mumble.

"Are you ready to come in, you two?" My mother

stands at the top of the beach, near the road, her cupped hands amplifying her voice.

"Not just yet," Dad says, winking at me. He takes off at a run, kicking sand on me as I jump up, chasing after him. I can hear my mother laughing behind us. The sandy beach gives way to pebbles and bigger rock formations, and soon neither of us is running as we pick our paths through wave-worn rocks. Mom and the road and the beach are far behind us. It's just me and Dad and the sea.

It's fake.

"No!" I say, just as my bare feet slip on the wet rock. I crash down, pain shooting up my scraped shin. Dad turns back and helps me up.

"Are you okay, Ella?" he asks.

No. NO.

"Yeah," I say.

"We shouldn't run," Dad says. "We should take the time to appreciate this area. You know where we are, right?"

I hadn't recognized it before, but now that Dad says it, I do know where I am. From the cliff above us extends a giant arm of rock, arcing over the sea and then reaching back down into the water. The rock formation has created a perfect arch—large enough to fit a house under—through which the sea flows. Waves crash against the sides of the rock, sending up salty sea foam.

"It's the Azure Window," I breathe, staring at this natural wonder.

It's not. Not really.

"Eyes are the window to the soul, Ella, don't forget that," Dad says. He's not looking at me; he's watching a girl swimming out in the ocean, so far away from us that I cannot recognize who she is.

"I... I thought the Azure Window was destroyed," I say slowly. "In the Secessionary War. The bombs broke the arch, the rock crumbled into the sea."

As I say the words, the natural bridge of rock cracks with an earsplitting snap. First pebbles, then boulders fall from the arch. The water churns with the destruction. Giant clouds of dirt and debris mar my vision of the crumbling rock formation. When the dust finally clears, there is nothing there but a pile of rocks and swirling, dirty water.

I turn to my father.

He's dead.

He's dead.

As I watch, the skin of his face cracks, like the rock did, exposing red blood. His flesh falls away from his skull like pebbles crashing to the sea. A waterfall of cascading blood and gore falls from his head, down his neck. His shoulder chips away, and, with a giant crash, the flesh from his chest falls from his body, an avalanche splattering into the sea at our feet, now stained red. I can see, for just a moment, his beating heart in his ribcage, and then that, too, withers and dies, the useless, blackened lump tapping against his ribs before plopping out of his body. He's nothing but bones, and then the gentle warm Mediterranean wind blows against him, and his bones break, clattering down into the pile of muck and flesh swirling in the salty sea.

"This isn't real," I say.

Because it isn't.

Chapter Two

I wake up with a violent jerk, running a shaky hand over my sleep-crusted eyes.

Ever since last year, the nightmares have been getting worse. More vivid. The line between what's real and what's not is so blurry.

Ever since I started working at the Reverie Mental Spa.

I sigh, throwing my blankets back and getting out of bed. By the time I make it to the kitchen, my mother's already slicing tomatoes for breakfast.

"Sleep well?" she asks cheerily.

"Yeah, no," I say, slumping into the chair. But when

she turns back to look at me, a curious smile on her lips, I just grin at her as if I'd woken up from the best dream ever.

Mom hands me the plate of tomatoes. "Forgot the basil," she mutters, turning away before the plate's fully in my hands.

They're real tomatoes, grown on our roof, not the perfect spheres from the market. Of course, they taste pretty much exactly like the genetically modified food the government stamps approval of sale on, but I like the weirdly discordant shapes of the tomatoes we grow ourselves. They're lumpier, as if they have only a vague idea of the round shape they're supposed to be. The rich, red insides glisten with the sprinkle of salt Mom threw over them before she handed them to me.

Then I notice the blood.

"Mom," I say evenly, trying not to make it sound like a big deal.

"Mmm?" she asks, not turning.

It's rather a lot of blood, mixed in with the slices. It's darker than the tomatoes' juice, smeared across the plate.

"Mom," I say again.

Mom turns, still holding the knife. I see the cut pulsing blood down her hand, cutting a dark path through the chopped green basil clinging to her skin. She's shorn off the tip of her second finger.

"Mom!" I say, dropping the plate on the counter and rushing to her. She looks down at her hand and curses, tossing the knife into the sink.

"Damn, damn, damn," she says. "It's ruined, isn't it?"

She looks past me at the plate of tomatoes. "All ruined. Damn!"

"I don't care about the tomatoes," I say, wrapping a tea towel around her finger as Mom reaches past me, grabbing the plate and sliding the tomato slices into the rubbish bin. "Be still," I order, but she doesn't listen. She tries to shake me off.

"Forget about the damn tomatoes!" I shout, snatching her hand again and pressing the towel into the cut. Mom stares down at it dispassionately, watching the red blood soak through the white cloth.

I slowly raise my eyes from Mom's hand to her face. There's no emotion on her face. No pain.

"You didn't feel it, did you?" I whisper.

"Of course I did," Mom says.

I squeeze the cut finger, just a little, just enough pressure that she should feel a spike of pain. But Mom doesn't notice.

I drop her hand, and Mom peels away the tea towel. It's ruined—but Mom's finger isn't. As we watch, the raw, bleeding flesh slowly knits back up, and the skin starts to regrow.

Mom snorts. "At least the bots are good for something."

"You're getting worse," I say. It's not a question.

"Ella—" Mom starts to reach for me, but I wrap my arms around myself. The back of my tongue aches as burning tears fill my eyes. "Ella, it's not that bad."

"It *is*!" I shout, staring at her. Mom's eyes plead with me to forget what I saw, to pretend that everything is okay. But it's not. It's not.

It's the beginning of the end.

This is the way things are:

Almost two years ago, Mom was diagnosed with Hebb's Disease. It's rare, and it's fatal. Some people think it comes from the universal cancer vaccination since it was developed a short time before the first case of the disease, but no one's sure. All we know is that, for some reason, the space between neurons starts to grow wider. Your brain is *yelling* at you to move, but your nervous system can't hear it.

Most people don't last more than half a year with Hebb's, but Mom's survived two whole years thanks to the research on nanobots Dad did. He was close to finding a cure, I know he was. He used nanobots to help alleviate the symptoms, using the tiny, microscopic robots to communicate the messages between Mom's brain and nervous system. The bots have the additional advantage to heal other areas where Mom's been hurt, like the cut on her finger. Medical nanobots are no new thing—everyone has vaccination bots when they're born—but the way Dad used them on Mom's illness... it seemed like a miracle.

But then Dad died.

And now Mom's...

Not being able to feel anything is the first warning sign. If a knife nearly sliced off her finger, and she didn't even freaking *notice*, that means Dad's temporary fix for Mom is failing. The bots aren't working. The disease is taking over. The disease that eventually kills every single one of its victims is winning.

"Mom," I say, my voice eerily calm. "How long have you had trouble feeling things?"

"It's not been long, Ella, please, don't worry about—"

"How long." It doesn't even sound like a question any more, just a demand.

Mom sighs. "A few months. It's... been getting steadily worse."

My hands are shaking so violently that I curl them into fists and hold them behind my back so Mom doesn't see. I can't be weak, not in front of her, not when she needs my strength.

When Mom was first diagnosed, I practiced saying "My mother is dead," until I could say it without crying.

And then Mom didn't die. Dad found a way to stave off the disease, and she lived.

But he didn't.

Dad's death was sudden, and violent, and it gutted me like knife guts a fish. An explosion in the lab where he worked, about a year ago, killing him and several other scientists. No one expected it—no one except the terrorists who planned it. I was so *angry*. He left me with a sick mother and no hope. And when I woke up the next morning, and every morning after, there would be a moment, a brief moment, where I'd forgotten Dad was dead. And every morning, I relived every ounce of pain when I remembered again that he wasn't here with us. With me.

"Ella." My mother speaks loudly, drawing me back to the here and now. "I don't want you to worry about it, really. Jadis is taking me to a new doctor, one of the ones in the lab that gave us the grant money, and well—don't give up hope on me, okay?"

I jerk my head up, staring at her fiercely. "Never," I say, and I mean it more than anything else I've ever sworn.

I'm not ready to be an orphan.

Beth Revis is the *New York Times* bestselling author of the Across the Universe trilogy, as well as the companion novel, *The Body Electric*. Her other novels include the Star Wars title *Rebel Rising*, a twisty contemporary *A World Without You*, and a dark fantasy *Give the Dark My Love*. Her next work is a serial novel entitled *Blood & Feathers*.

Her short stories have appeared in several anthologies and magazines. She currently lives in rural North Carolina with her husband, son, and dog.

For more from Beth:
www.bethrevis.com

Sign up for exclusive content & deals:
bethrevis.substack.com